LYDIE'S GHOST

LYDIE'S GHOST

A NOVEL BY

BOB PERRY

Lydie's Ghost

To our dear Sydney: gone, but never forgotten.

Thanks to Goldie Hagen for helping get this story told.

Special thanks to my Burnt Cabin campers that keep me filled with good dialogue and ideas each and every year.

CHAPTER 1

"I'm not telling you again!" Jordan Bennett's mother threatened. "Find your brother!"

Apathetically, Jordan Bennett rolled her eyes and asked, "Where's he at?"

Barbara Bennett had little patience with her daughter that afternoon. It had been a hard year for the family and Barbara could not understand Jordan's stubborn defiance.

"I don't know, Jordan," Barbara Bennett sighed. "But I want him here before I go to work."

Jordan did not argue, but stomped out in silent protest of her mother interrupting her television show. The hot August evening made Jordan sigh heavily. She would have preferred to stay in front of the fan that had been cooling her. The twelve-year-old Jordan should have felt guilty about making her mother ask her three times to do the simple job of finding her brother Brett, but she received some secret satisfaction from aggravating her mother.

The sun caused Jordan to squint as she looked down the empty 13th Street. She had no idea where her brother might be, but knew he had to be within walking distance. Her brother Brett was two years older than she was and still two years away from driving. Jordan's family had moved to Ponca City from Stillwater the previous fall. Jordan had been happy in Stillwater. She liked her school, the familiar house, and her best friend Chloe Beck, who still lived there. Her family moved because her mother had thought it would be a good opportunity. Jordan's dad had not wanted to come, but her mother pushed and nagged her father into moving. Stillwater was less than sixty miles away, but Jordan felt as if it were a thousand.

Thirteenth Street in Ponca City was far from a bad part of town, but Jordan's house was the smallest on the block. Her family lived in the only rent house in the neighborhood and Jordan always felt as if they did not belong. Jordan had believed living on 13th Street was ominous when they moved, but she could not have imagined how badly things would go for her family there. The year 1986 promised good times in Ponca City, but the town's prosperity did not include Jordan's family.

Her father's work took him out of town often when they first moved. After a while, Jordan's father was gone more than he was at home until one day he left for good. Jordan blamed her mother for making him so unhappy. After he left, her mother worked part-time and enrolled in the local vocational school to become a nurse. Jordan and her only brother Brett were on their own most nights. Jordan's life raged with uncertainty bordering on despair. She did not understand her life and everything she once trusted seemed to be slipping away.

As Jordan roamed the lonely street looking for signs of her brother, she passed Mr. Grumman's house on the corner. The neighborhood boys called him Mr. Grumpy and his small red brick house with aluminum foil over the windows was known by all the kids as Grumpy Old Man Corner. Mr. Grumman's yard was neater than most, but a high wood fence hid the backyard from view. Kids in the neighborhood stayed clear of the place, although some of the boys would sometimes knock on the door and run on a dare. There was something ominous about the house to Jordan. Although Jordan had rarely seen Mr. Grumman, she always walked more quickly when passing his place.

Across 14th Street, Jordan scanned a small shopping center featuring a Safeway grocery store, a TG&Y variety store, and a Walgreens drugstore with a fountain. Brett sometimes did odd jobs for the manager of the TG&Y who hired him to cut down boxes. Jordan scampered across the busy 14th Street to the alley behind the TG&Y, but no one had seen Brett that afternoon. Jordan looked down the alley and believed she knew where to find her brother.

Jordan crossed a busy street before heading across a circle drive encompassing a twenty foot tall statue called The Pioneer Woman. The statue depicted a stoic and determined woman in a long dress leading a young boy by the hand. The imposing sculpture guarded the entrance to a more prosperous neighborhood up Monument Road. The woman in the statue reminded Jordan of her mother, causing her to hurry past an older couple taking photographs of the figure.

Surrounded by nicely manicured yards and spacious homes, Monument Road ran at an uphill angle from the statue. Jordan moved quickly up the road focusing her eyes on her shoes most of the way. The young girl believed residents in this part of town would not like her intrusion, although she had walked the street many times.

At the top of the hill, a pair of formidable stone pillars held sturdy, wrought iron gates guarding a castle-like mansion on the top of the hill. Jordan walked quickly through the gate, her long legs causing her to bounce awkwardly. She was a slender girl, but Jordan saw herself as too skinny. Her shoulder-length brown hair had been blonde the summer before when her family lived in Stillwater. Jordan had loved her blonde hair. She did not like the change in hair color and did not like other changes in her life that seemed to torment her.

The sun began the transition from afternoon to evening as it glowed against the formidable, stone mansion. Sunbeams caused her to squint as she looked to the west. There was no sign of her brother inside the gates.

The property had once been a Catholic school, but the city purchased the mansion and converted the old dormitories into a hotel with meeting rooms. Although the property was public, Jordan felt as if she were trespassing when she came there. Her brother Brett, however, did not share her timidity about the place. An open field, a large pond, and a secluded section of dense woods nearby drew Brett and his friends to the place. Jordan had found him many times playing near the mansion.

As Jordan walked east around the building, her shadow bobbed in front of her, exaggerating her long arms and legs. Jordan was self-conscious about much of her appearance, but particularly her bony elbows, which she constantly tried to hide by keeping her arms to her side or folding them across her chest. Her self-conscious attempts to conceal her slender frame made her gait even more awkward. Jordan turned to admire the stately mansion to avoid watching her own shadow.

The Marland Mansion, as everyone in town called it, was a magnificent structure. The terra cotta tiled roof and rough stone

walls glowed in the sun. Jordan could see a large outdoor balcony overlooking a clover shaped piece of lawn. Her brother's friends had told her that the clover shape had once been a swimming pool, but Jordan had a hard time believing any pool could be of such a size. The three story mansion was crowned with at least five chimneys she could see. Jordan thought the huge house looked like a castle. As Jordan rounded the east side of the large house, she was startled by the screeching of a scrawny cat crossing her path.

"Watch where you're going!" demanded a strange old woman who sat on one of the many steps leading to the large mansion.

"I'm sorry," Jordan muttered.

"What are you doing here?" the old woman pointedly asked.

"I—I," Jordan stammered.

Jordan was mesmerized by the odd-looking woman sitting a few feet away who questioned her. The frail, old woman looked commanding to the timid Jordan. She wore an old raincoat, although there was not a cloud in the sky and the temperature was quite warm. Several tattered scarves decorated the base of her wrinkled neck like a necklace. The woman's eyes were brown and shifted nervously as if watching for some unseen predator to pounce. Her voice was calm and precise.

"Speak up," the old woman demanded.

"I'm looking for my brother," Jordan finally answered.

"Brother?" the old woman asked.

Jordan nodded silently. She was afraid of the old woman, although the woman had to be a head shorter than she was and nearly eighty years old. Before Jordan could think of anything else to say, she let out a muffled screech as the thin cat rubbed against her bare ankle.

Collecting her thoughts, Jordan reached down to pet the sable colored cat with its lean, hungry face and asked, "Is this your cat?"

"Cats don't belong to anyone," the woman answered in a very precise tone.

"Oh," Jordan timidly responded.

The old woman studied Jordan carefully before adding, "She lives with me—we live with each other."

Jordan reached down again to pet the cat, as the feline scampered away.

"You said you had a brother?" the old woman asked again.

"Yes ma'am," Jordan replied.

The old woman did not respond, but her stern gaze seemed to soften at the girl's polite response.

"My mother sent me to look for my brother," Jordan explained. "He sometimes plays around here."

"Where do you live?" the old woman asked suspiciously.

When Jordan instinctively moved her fingers to her mouth, the old woman barked, "Don't bite your fingernails!"

Jordan looked at her stubby fingernails, which she routinely chewed when nervous and replied, "Sorry, ma'am."

"Don't be sorry to me," the old woman instructed. "I would love to have beautiful hands like yours and I hate to see a young girl mistreat her nails like that."

Jordan nodded obediently.

"You didn't tell me where you live," the woman restated.

Jordan refrained from biting her nails and answered, "On 13th Street, just south of Lake Drive."

The old woman looked over her shoulder to the south as if determining the distance, although the mansion blocked any possible view.

"How old is your brother?" the woman asked.

"Fourteen," Jordan replied.

"And you?" the woman quizzed.

"Twelve," Jordan answered.

This response changed the old woman's demeanor. She struggled to pull herself from her seat and stepped toward Jordan. The old woman's shoulders stooped, but Jordan noticed she had an unmistakable grace to her walk.

"An older brother," the old woman said with a raised eyebrow.

"Yes."

The old woman studied Jordan for a moment before asking in a friendlier tone, "You're not from around here?"

"No," Jordan smiled. "How did you know?"

"I've lived a long time and know most of the snoops around here," the woman stated. "I saw some young men down by the lake behind the mansion. You might find your brother there."

"Thank you," Jordan said, as she headed in the direction the woman suggested.

Jordan had walked about forty steps when she turned to look back at the old woman, but to her surprise, the woman had vanished.

CHAPTER 2

Something about the old woman intrigued Jordan. She assumed the strange woman had stepped around the building out of sight. Jordan shrugged and continued searching for her brother.

As Jordan walked around the house toward an open field, an oddly dressed man startled her. The man, who was wearing a dark suit and carrying a black walking stick, looked sternly at her. A panicked Jordan trotted away from the stranger, hoping to find her brother behind the mansion.

Jordon stopped running when she saw several boys throwing a baseball in a large open field close to a small lake. Her brother Brett batted balls to other boys out in the field, but Jordan's attention quickly turned to Brett's friend J.J. Reynolds. Jordan sighed as she watched J.J. slap his glove and move gracefully to scoop up a ground ball before tossing it effortlessly to one of the other boys. J.J.'s sandy hair moved in concert with his lean body while his tanned face framed blue eyes. Jordan could not see his blue eyes from this distance, but she had studied them carefully other times. Looking behind her, Jordan no longer saw the man who had frightened her earlier.

Jordan leaned against a rock wall overlooking the field where she inconspicuously watched the boys. The wall framed three elegant arches sheltering an area that looked like an outdoor patio that went into the hill. Somebody told her the structure was a boathouse, but a walkway overhead made the building look more like a bridge. Jordan had little interest in the architecture. The spot provided a place for her to watch the boys without being noticed.

J.J. looked up at her once, but to Jordan's disappointment he did not smile or acknowledge her. Jordan was too shy to interrupt her brother, although she knew her mother would be unhappy at her delay. Time had little meaning to her as she watched the boys, although she knew their game would not have held her interest without J.J.'s presence.

Jordan's heart jumped when she felt the furry rub of a cat on her ankle.

"The cat likes you," a voice stated from behind Jordan. "That's funny, because she doesn't like most people."

Jordan glanced around to see the odd old woman she had met earlier standing several feet away, while the cat hummed a throaty purr.

"I see you found him," the old woman said.

Jordan turned to face the woman and muttered, "Huh?"

"Your brother," the woman replied. "I see you found your brother."

"Yes ma'am," Jordan answered. "Thank you."

The woman stood several inches shorter than the young girl. Jordan studied the old woman's odd wardrobe and noticed the woman's red and rough-looking hands. Jordan looked a little too long and the woman discreetly moved her hands behind her back.

"Which one is he?" the woman asked.

Jordan turned around to study the field before saying, "The one in the green shirt."

The old woman smiled, revealing several teeth missing before covering her mouth with her red hands. Jordan believed the woman giggled, but the response seemed so out of character with her earlier conversation that the young girl believed she must be mistaken.

Tightening her lips and hiding her hands once again, the old woman asked, "One of the boys has your attention?"

"No," Jordan instinctively answered. "I'm just watching the game."

"What's the score?" the old woman asked.

Jordan's only response was a befuddled stare.

"What's the boy's name?" the old woman asked.

"What boy?" Jordan answered.

"The good looking boy wearing the red shirt with a number 44 on it," the old woman replied.

Jordan was somewhat surprised and miffed that the old woman had deduced she was watching J.J. Reynolds instead of the ball game.

"How did you know?" Jordan asked.

The woman grunted to herself and said, "I haven't always been old. Are you going to tell me his name or continue pretending you're not interested?"

Jordan felt confused and relieved at the opportunity to say, "J.J. Reynolds."

Jordan continued nervously, "He's just a friend of my brother."

"Just a friend of your brother," the woman restated.

The old woman looked at the boys on the field as if looking at another time and place before adding, "My brother had a handsome friend when I was twelve. I remember what it's like to have a boy that's 'just a friend of your brother.'"

Jordan listened to the woman in awkward silence before asking, "What was his name?"

"Why would you want to know that?" the woman replied brusquely.

"I—I," Jordan stammered at the unexpected response from the old woman.

"Did you talk to that man?" the old woman charged.

"What man?" Jordan asked.

"That man snooping about spying on me!" the agitated woman asserted. "Did he ask you to find out?"

"No ma'am," a helpless Jordan replied. "I saw a man earlier, but I ran away...I ran as fast as I could."

The old woman looked around, stretching her wrinkled neck surveying the area. Jordan's response seemed to satisfy her and the woman became calm as quickly as she had become annoyed.

"You saw the man, too?" the old woman asked in a more pleasant tone. "It's good that you didn't talk to him. Be careful of strangers...especially in this town."

"Yes ma'am," Jordan nodded.

"I always liked names that were initials," the old woman said. "What's your name?"

"Jordan."

"Jordan?" the old woman frowned. "Sounds like a boy's name. What's your middle name?"

"Louise," Jordan offered.

"J.L.," the old woman mused. "That's not a good name for initials, although I always liked the name Louise. What's J.J. stand for?"

Jordan hesitated an instant before answering, "I don't know."

The old woman restrained a smile with her tight, thin lips and said, "Maybe you should find out."

Jordan nodded slightly, but felt silly watching a boy for such a long time without knowing anything about him other than his initials.

"Looks like the boys are done," the old woman noted as she looked past Jordan.

Jordan turned around to see several boys pushing each other as if they had been in an argument. A couple of boys headed to their homes north of the mansion.

Jordan turned around to ask the old woman her name, but the woman walked away from her. As Jordan looked back to the field, she made eye contact with her brother. Brett walked slowly toward her. To Jordan's thrill and horror, J.J. Reynolds followed him.

CHAPTER 3

As J.J. Reynolds and Brett approached, Jordan tried to hide her bony elbows and big toothed smile, while hoping her knees would not visibly knock together.

"What are you doing here?" Brett bluntly asked.

"Mom sent me," Jordan answered.

"I'll be home in a while," Brett shrugged.

"She wants you home before she goes to work," Jordan informed him.

Brett looked at the sun, which was now low in the sky and said, "It's too late for that."

Jordan frowned, knowing she had been gone longer than her mother would have liked. The frown turned into twisted angst as Jordan realized her mother might be driving their beat-up old car to look for them. Barbara Bennett worked part-time at a local convenience store and liked to have her children home before she left for work. Brett, however, had routinely been out past dark to the frustration of his mother.

"We need to get home, just the same," Jordan pleaded.

Brett looked at his younger sister and said in a kinder tone, "Go on. I'll come home in a minute...I'll be home before dark."

"There's nothing left to do here," J.J. Reynolds interjected. "I might as well get home, too. I'll walk with you."

Without thinking, Jordan blurted out, "Can I come?"

The boys looked at the awkward girl a moment before J.J. said, "There's only one street that leads to your house. We can't keep you off it."

Jordan was disappointed in the young man's indifference, but looked forward to walking with him as far as her house. J.J. Reynolds lived somewhere closer to downtown. Jordan did not know anything about his family or home, but she always had the impression that J.J. was a little rebellious and even wild.

"I'll come too," Brad Cooper added.

Brad Cooper was another friend of Brett Bennett. Brad was average in every way with short brown hair, understated clothes, and a freckled, round face. The only distinctive thing about Brad Cooper was his nickname, Coop. All of Brett's friends had nicknames. There was a small boy they called Peanut and an even smaller boy they called Munchkin. Another friend, Ben Klein, was a large, good natured boy they all called Gump. Jordan could never get used to the other boys calling her brother B.B. instead of Brett.

"It's not on your way home, Coop," J.J. noted.

"I know," Brad Cooper replied, "but I've got nothing better to do."

J.J. Reynolds shrugged his shoulders and headed south toward Monument Road, which led away from the mansion. Brett followed him while Brad Cooper closed ranks on the other side. Jordan stood motionless for a moment before walking quickly to catch up with Brett, J.J., and Brad Cooper.

Eager to be involved in the boys' conversation, Jordan asked, "Did you see that old woman earlier?"

"What woman?" Brett asked.

"The woman talking to me at your game," Jordan explained.

"I didn't see no woman," Brett replied.

"She was there!" Jordan insisted.

"So," Brett scolded. "Who cares about an old woman? Quit trying to be a pest...I mean quit being a pest."

"I saw her, Jordan," Brad Cooper interjected. "She was standing with you."

"Is that why you dropped the ball, Coop?" J.J. Reynolds teased.

"No," Brad defended. "I told you, the sun got in my eyes."

"Couldn't keep your eyes off B.B.'s sister is more like it," J.J. smirked.

"I told you it was an old woman I saw," Brad replied. "Jordan just happened to be standing there."

"What do you think, Jor...DAN," J.J. mocked, as he exaggerated the "dan" portion of Jordan's name.

Before Jordan could think of a witty reply, Brett said, "This is why I don't want you around. You cause nothing but trouble. No one wants to hear about some old woman who'll listen to your dumb stories."

"Maybe it wasn't an old woman at all," J.J. said seriously. "Maybe it was a ghost."

"Right," Brett grunted.

"No, really," J.J. coaxed, as the four walked in front of the mansion and toward the imposing iron gate. "I've heard stories about this place. They said the old man that lived here killed his wife so he could marry a younger woman. It was in all the papers. He did the old lady in but she cursed him and he lost all his money...the mansion...and even the woman."

"Bull!" Brett grumbled.

"Really," J.J. insisted. "People say the place is haunted. My cousin used to be a security guard here and he said weird stuff happened all the time. It's full of secret passages, gargoyles, spy holes...I've even heard people say you can hear the place moan at midnight. I've been inside. Ask Coop."

"We've been inside," Brad Cooper admitted. "But I don't know about that other stuff."

"When have you been inside?" Brett challenged.

"Sixth grade," J.J. boasted. "We took a field trip. You didn't live here then."

"It's true," Brad added.

"Come look at this," J.J. said, while walking around to the front of the house.

J.J. pointed at a small carving that looked like a devil's head with an evil smile and horns on top of its head. The wicked-looking image was placed in a recess under the large portico.

"See!" J.J. challenged. "Who would put this creepy looking thing on the front of their house?"

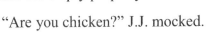

"I don't think we're supposed to be here," Brett reasoned, as he looked around the empty property.

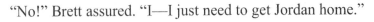

"Are you chicken?" J.J. mocked.

"No!" Brett assured. "I—I just need to get Jordan home."

"Oooh," J.J. replied. "The little girl's getting scared."

"I'm not scared," Jordan interjected.

"You should be," J.J. smugly said. "I'll tell you the story if you promise not to cry."

Jordan nodded meekly, while Brett and Brad stepped close to hear the story.

"Years ago," J.J. began, "a man and his wife lived in this house all alone. No children—nobody—just the two of them in the house all alone. Some say the man went crazy and killed his wife with a pair of clipping shears from the gardener. They say at midnight you can hear her moan on a still night. A reporter from the newspaper tried to stay the night a few years back and he heard the organ play itself, things moved around for no reason...and weirdest of all...the picture of the woman in the mansion was cut across the throat with blood dripping on the floor. Be real quiet and listen. You might hear the moan even now."

Jordan and the other boys became deathly quiet as they leaned to listen for anything out of the ordinary.

Jordan's forehead wrinkled in concentration when she heard a blood-curdling shriek, "Aagh!"

Jordan screamed and dashed a few steps away from the empty house before hearing the disturbing laughter from J.J. and the other boys.

"You're such a dweeb," Brett scolded, as his sister blushed in embarrassment. "He just told you the story from *The Ghost and Mr. Chicken* and you bought it hook, line, and sinker."

"I knew he was teasing," Jordan defended herself.

"Sure you did, JorDAN," J.J. mocked. "That's why you ran."

Jordan did not respond, but took her ridicule in silence and fell in line behind the boys as they walked away from the house and toward Monument Road.

The boys were laughing and ignoring Jordan when J.J. said, "You going with me and Coop tomorrow night, B.B.? We can make a little money."

Brett looked uneasy and tried to signal his friends to ask later.

"What?" J.J. asked.

"Don't talk in front of her," Brett protested. "She can't keep her mouth shut."

"Keep my mouth shut about what?" Jordan quizzed.

"None of your business!" Brett replied.

"Sorry, man," J.J. said. "I'll catch you tomorrow."

As the group passed the iron gate, Jordan heard a distinctive screeching sound that scared her much more than any story about a haunted mansion. Jordan wanted to hide, as she watched her mother's decrepit car clank toward them.

Jordan's heart sank. She knew her mother would not be happy at her delay. Brett and Jordan's mother peered underneath the driver's side visor that hung limply at an angle. The 1978 Dodge Omni had seen better days, but Jordan could not imagine it. The car was putty colored with streaks of rust along the lower part of the body. Their mother called the car dependable, but it made a hideous clanking sound. Jordan thought the car ugly and embarrassing. She had started asking her mother to let her out a block from the junior high on the days her mother drove her to school so the other girls would not laugh at her.

Barbara Bennett looked angry. Her straight brown hair was wind-blown and her pale, plain face looked tired. The air conditioning in the car had quit working a month earlier and she had decided to wait until next summer to have it fixed.

"I'll see you guys," Brett said meekly as he trotted to meet his mother.

Jordan did not say anything as she slowly followed.

"Tomorrow?" J.J. asked.

"I'll see," Brett answered, but he nodded slightly at the two boys to indicate he would be with them.

Brett sat in front with his mother, while Jordan slumped in the back seat that was cluttered with books and papers from her mother's school.

Jordan expected to be scolded, but her mother just sighed wearily and said, "I've got to go to work. Can you fix your own supper tonight?"

"Sure, Mom," Brett replied. "I'll take care of Jordan, too."

His mother forced a smile and drove to their small home less than four blocks away. The past year had been tense between Jordan and her mother, but Brett always seemed to be at peace with his mother. Barbara Bennett rarely criticized Brett like she was apt to do with her daughter. Jordan had been a daddy's girl and Jordan believed her mother resented her for that. Brett had more empathy for his mother, and he seemed to be the one joy left in her increasingly challenging life.

Barbara Bennett had never worked until three years ago and now she was desperate to find a better job for herself and her children. She worked the evening shift at a convenience store, but was trying to go to school to become a nurse. She would go to school every day and then usually work seven to midnight on Tuesdays, Thursdays, and Fridays plus an eight hour shift on Saturdays. Most other evenings she did clinical hours at the hospital or one of the care facilities. Sundays were her only day of rest, and even on that day she managed church, cleaning, and the laundry.

"Be good," Barbara Bennett admonished her children as she drove off leaving them in the front yard alone.

"What are you doing tomorrow?" Jordan asked her brother once they were alone.

"None of your business," Brett replied, as he headed inside to warm up the stew leftover from the night before.

"Come on," Jordan pleaded. "I might want to go."

"No!" Brett barked.

"I'll tell Mom," Jordan threatened.

Brett's face flushed with anger, before regaining his composure and saying, "Tell her what?"

Jordan thought about Brett's logic. All she knew was that Brett had some plans for the next day. She did not know what her brother was up to and she did not even know what time the unmentioned event was supposed to take place. She did know that J.J. Reynolds planned to be there and that was enough to keep her interest.

"Nothing," Jordan admitted.

Before heading to the kitchen to heat up some stew, Brett looked at his sister to make sure he had made his point about her keeping out of his business. Jordan did not question him further, but she was stubbornly determined to keep an eye on her brother the next day.

CHAPTER 4

Jordan endured the first week of school. While the popular kids at East Junior High went home with parents in car pools, an anxious Jordan was herded onto a school bus each afternoon. Although Jordon did not want her mother coming to school in their old car, she felt like an outcast on the bus.

No other girls lived on her street, so Jordan sat alone when the bus stopped a block from her house. Jordan walked quickly by Grumpy Old Man Corner where a grouchy old man lived. He often peered out his front window at any children that might step on his immaculately mowed lawn. Although Jordan had never actually seen the man, she watched carefully to make sure he was not leering at her. After passing the corner house, Jordan walked in solitude, enjoying a few minutes of peace until her mother came home.

The small front room of the Bennett house was clean, but cluttered. Jordan's mother spent every Sunday afternoon cleaning, but by Friday things were out of order again.

Until two years ago, Jordan's mother had always been home when she arrived. Brett attended Ponca City High School; the students called it Po Hi. He came home about fifteen minutes after Jordan and Barbara Bennett usually made it home by 4:15. Jordan sometimes felt lonely and neglected when home alone. It was a painful reminder that her father was not home. Today, however, she was content to go to her room and enjoy not fighting with her mother for a few minutes.

Barbara Bennett sighed heavily when she entered the house and forced a smile when greeting her children. She asked Brett to stay home this evening and Jordan just grunted when her mother asked how her day had been. Barbara would go to work a little before seven and would be gone until after eleven o'clock. Barbara was surprised when Brett agreed to watch Jordan without a fuss, but it was Friday and there was a level of peace that came with the weekend.

Jordan ate supper in silence, but carefully watched her brother, who was being too cooperative. Jordan could not believe her mother's lack of suspicion, but Jordan knew something was up and she was determined to find out what it was. After her mother left for work, Jordan settled in to watch *Dallas*. Brett would typically fight her for control of the television on Friday nights because he preferred the action of *Miami Vice*. His strategy almost worked, as Jordan focused on her show and almost failed to notice the squeak of the front door as it closed behind Brett.

Jordan looked out the front window and watched her brother walk north. She hurriedly put on her shoes and followed. The air was warm and muggy. The sun had set, but dusk provided enough faint light to keep Brett in view.

Jordan's curiosity turned to concern as she watched him walk seriously and purposefully.

Jordan remembered J.J. Reynolds telling her brother they could make some money. J.J. had a reputation around town and Jordan worried about her brother. She had heard about drugs and wondered if her brother were involved in something illicit. Brett had always been responsible, but that was before their father left them.

Brett headed up Monument Road with Jordan tagging behind, just barely keeping him in sight. As Brett approached the iron gate to the mansion, he moved away from the public entrance and slid underneath a gap in the iron and stone fence surrounding the mansion. J.J. Reynolds and Brad Cooper joined Brett inside the fence. Jordan moved quickly underneath the fence and hid in the shadows. She was afraid someone might spot her, but she was more afraid of being found out by the boys. She peered from her hiding spot to see the boys having a serious discussion.

As it became darker the boys headed south of the hotel along the rock wall and toward a thickly wooded area to the east. Jordan kept the boys in sight, but they were moving faster now. They entered the woods and Jordan was determined to find out their mystery. As she approached the woods, Jordan looked up the hill to see the hotel staff preparing for some kind of party on the mansion grounds. A band was setting up and Jordan assumed it was a reception from one of the many weddings held there. Jordan stepped into the thick woods and tried to follow a narrow, dark trail the boys had taken.

She could not see the boys, but she could hear them talking in muffled tones. After a few minutes, Jordan was lost. There was barely enough light from the nearly full moon to see the path she had taken and she could not see the hotel or mansion behind her. She had no choice but to follow the boys and head deeper into the darkness. One of the boys had a flashlight and she was able to keep them in sight. In a few more minutes, Jordan came to an opening in the small forest and was surprised to come upon a street. It took a moment to recognize where she was, but the boys had walked to a residential area on the other side of the woods. The boys walked quickly through the neighborhood, and Jordan found it harder to follow without being seen. The boys crossed Pecan Street and jumped over a barbed wire fence to an open, mowed field. Jordan watched carefully as J.J. and her brother stripped off their shirts in the pale moonlight.

"What are you doing here?" a startled voice from Brad Cooper whispered from the darkness.

Jordan squealed loud enough to attract the attention of J.J. and Brett who stood across the road.

The two boys looked nervously into the darkness before Brad Cooper said, "It's okay. It's just Jordan."

J.J. looked relieved, but Brett put his shirt back on and jumped over the fence to confront his sister who was now standing next to Brad Cooper.

"What are you doing here?" Brett angrily whispered.

"What am I doing here?" Jordan responded. "What are you doing here?"

The question rattled Brett who was only able to mutter something about her spying on him.

"They're swimming for balls," Brad Cooper explained.

"What?" Jordan asked.

"They're swimming for balls on the golf course," Brad continued.

"You're supposed to be at home," Brett scolded in a loud whisper.

"So are you," Jordan shot back.

Brett fumed while Brad said, "Don't worry, I'll watch out for her."

"She'll ruin everything!" Brett replied.

"No she won't," Brad tried to assure him. "You won't tell, will you Jordan?"

Jordan shook her head, somewhat relieved that her brother was not involved in a more clandestine activity.

"She does and she's had it!" Brett threatened.

Across the road, J.J. Reynolds whistled and signaled Brett to rejoin him. Brett gave his sister one more threatening look and headed back over the fence.

"Why are you guys out here?" Jordan questioned after her brother had left.

"The guys sneak onto the golf course on nights when there's moonlight," Brad explained. "They get in the ponds and feel for lost balls. There's a guy that will pay fifteen cents a ball. On a good night, they can get 200 balls out of the water."

"Oh," Jordan replied. "How come you're not with them?"

"My dad and I play at that course," Brad explained. "He'd ground me for life if I got caught. I come to watch out for them and keep close to the woods so I can run if I have to. I also make sure J.J. doesn't do something stupid that might get him into trouble. There's also leeches in the water and I can't deal with that."

"Is getting the balls illegal?" Jordan asked.

Brad shrugged his shoulders and replied, "I don't know. I doubt it's a crime to get the balls, they are lost after all. They're probably trespassing, though. You guys aren't members of the Country Club are you?"

"No," Jordan affirmed.

Brad seemed content to keep Jordan company, but after she determined that Brett was not going to get into any real trouble she said, "I got to get back."

"Through those woods in the dark?" Brad chuckled. "Lots of luck."

"Is there another way?" Jordan asked.

"Sure," Brad replied. "If you go by the road, though, it's about two miles."

Looking at the skinny girl for a second, Brad said, "Come on. I've got a flashlight and I'll take you back the way we came. It's shorter."

Brad led Jordan through the neighborhood across from the golf course. They snuck through the backyard of one of the houses and into the thick woods. Brad held back limbs to help the girl along the dark trail.

"Don't go that way," Brad instructed as Jordan walked ahead of him. "You'll get lost."

"What's down there?" Jordan asked.

Brad shrugged and said, "I don't really know. The terrain is rough…too rough to walk through in the dark. J.J. says there's some caves further in the woods, but I don't know. If you walk far enough, there is an old woman with a farmhouse by Lake Road. J.J. and Gump wandered too far one afternoon and the old woman fired a shotgun over their heads."

"Really?" Jordan quizzed.

"Probably," Brad replied. "Gump told me that story. I trust his story more than J.J.'s."

After Brad pointed the way, the two quickly made it back to the large mowed field next to the mansion and hotel.

"I can walk you home," Brad offered as they emerged from the trees.

"I can make it," Jordan assured him. "Do you know the time?"

Looking at his watch, Brad said, "About eight-thirty."

"Thanks," Jordan nodded as Brad headed back into the woods.

Jordan took a deep breath, knowing she needed to get home before her mother found out she had left the house. The evening was comfortable, with a hint of coolness to the air. Jordan heard a band playing at the wedding reception at the mansion. She looked to see lights strung on poles to the east of the large house and the band playing on a raised platform. A couple of hundred people enjoyed the jazzy music, as they carried on their hum of conversation.

Outside the glow of the artificial lights, a strange image caught Jordan's attention. She did not know what to make of the aberration at first. Jordan watched a woman dancing in the darkness with the moonlight glowing off a flowing white dress. The partygoers did not seem to notice the odd sight, but Jordan could not take her eyes off the strange scene.

Jordan turned around to see if Brad Cooper was still standing close by so she could ask if he was seeing the same thing. Brad was gone, but Jordan turned to look at the woman once again. She could not believe it at first, but as she looked closer she could tell that the moonlight dancer was the old woman she had seen around the mansion the previous afternoon. Her faithful cat curled a few feet away watching the old woman sway to the music.

The old woman appeared oblivious to her surroundings as she danced to the rhythmic music coming from the band. Jordan looked at the people at the party to see that no one detected her lonesome waltz. As Jordan turned to watch the woman again, she saw nothing but a dark portion of the lawn. The woman had vanished, as if she knew someone was watching. Jordan scanned the area once more, but could not see the old woman she had seen dancing in the darkness. The band finished their song and Jordan decided it was time to head home.

It took the girl a little less than fifteen minutes to make the walk in the dark. Jordan nervously entered the empty house and quickly checked all the rooms to make sure she was alone. She locked the doors and turned on the television to watch a new science fiction series. Jordan was relieved to see Brett come in a little before ten o'clock.

"How many balls did you find?" a sassy Jordan asked.

Her brother Brett did not answer, he just stared at his sister.

"Don't worry," Jordan assured him. "I won't tell Mom."

Brett had started toward the bathroom to take a shower, when he stopped and said, "We fished out thirty dollars worth of balls."

Jordan's mother arrived a few minutes later. She tried to engage Jordan in conversation, but the young girl was not in the mood and Barbara Bennett was too tired. Jordan's mother went to bed and Brett stayed in his room, leaving Jordan alone to watch a late night movie. Jordan thought about the strange woman she had seen dancing in the darkness and wondered why no one else noticed. Jordan watched her late movie and soon forgot about the old woman at the mansion.

CHAPTER 5

"Jordan!" Barbara Bennett scolded. "Don't tell me you slept in that chair all night."

Jordan groggily rubbed her eyes and listened to the dull conversation of a Saturday morning infomercial before replying, "Okay, I won't."

Barbara was not in the mood to listen to her daughter's smart replies, as she said, "Don't use that tone with me...and don't you roll those eyes."

"It's not a big deal," Jordan whined. "It's not like I'm out getting in trouble."

"That's not the point," Barbara Bennett replied. "I could use a little help around here and you staying up all hours does not help."

"I'm up now," Jordan shot back.

With a sigh, her mother said, "Only because I came into the room to see that you stayed up late enough to fall asleep in front of the television. I want you to clean up this place today and make yourself useful."

Jordan did not reply as she flipped through television channels to find something to watch.

In a few moments, Barbara Bennett walked back through the front room on her way out and said, "I'm not kidding, Jordan. I want you to pick up things this morning."

Jordan nodded unenthusiastically, as her mother headed out the door. Brett got a call from the TG&Y discount store on 14th Street and headed out to do some odd jobs for them. Jordan settled into her comfortable chair to watch the *Bugs Bunny / Looney Tunes Comedy Hour*. The morning slipped by and Jordan forgot about her mother's instructions to clean house until she heard the ominous clanking of her mother's car in the driveway as she returned home for a lunch break.

Jordan jumped to her feet and hurriedly tried to straighten up the clutter in the front room, but she was not even able to get her breakfast bowl put away before the door opened. Jordan's mother did not say anything for a second, but her disapproving look caused Jordan's cheeks to flush pink.

"Is it too much to ask for you to help me…a little?" Barbara Bennett sighed.

"I was getting to it," Jordan explained.

"Well—you'll have plenty of time," Barbara declared. "You're grounded."

"That's not fair!" Jordan protested. "I'm supposed to go see Chloe next week!"

"Life's not fair," her mother assured her.

"You're ruining my life!" Jordan screamed.

"Don't be so dramatic," Barbara Bennett replied.

"But what about Chloe?" Jordan cried.

Barbara Bennett looked strangely at her daughter and said, "I'm sorry, but I wasn't going to be able to take you to Chloe's anyway. Maybe she can visit sometime."

"Dad would take me!" Jordan snapped.

"I'm sorry, dear, but your dad won't—" her mother tried to explain.

"I know why Dad left you!" Jordan screamed. "You can't stand for any of us to be happy if you're not happy!"

Barbara Bennett stared silently at her daughter. She fought back emotions of anger and regret. Barbara often wondered if she could have handled things differently, but that was in the past. She had tried her best to keep her family together. Her son Brett seemed to understand, but she knew Jordan blamed her.

"You don't know everything," Barbara tried to explain. "Things aren't always what they seem. Your daddy didn't leave me, he left us."

"That's not true!" Jordan angrily replied. "Daddy would still be here if you hadn't always griped at him and made him miserable."

Jordan's father, Randle Bennett, had moved out six months earlier and Jordan had not seen him in weeks. Jordan's father was a barrel-chested man in his thirties that still had a boyish grin and a playful nature. He had moved his family from

Stillwater two years earlier for a new start, but things had not gone well. Randle had been an oilfield worker, but those jobs had been hard to find. He worked as a maintenance man at the refinery for a while, but did not like being tied down to regular hours. He took a job driving a truck that took him away from the house most nights. After a while, he spent more and more time away from home as the fights between himself and his wife became more regular.

"I'm not going to argue with you," Barbara Bennett said, as she tried to steady her voice. "I have to grab a bite to eat and get back to work. I want his house clean when I get back."

"I won't be here!" Jordan fumed as she stormed to her room and slammed the door shut.

The sound of her daughter banging the door was too much for Barbara to ignore. She had tried to keep her composure, but her daughter had managed to frustrate her.

Barbara Bennett knocked on the door and said sternly, "I won't have you talk to me like that. I deserve a little respect around here."

Jordan did not answer, but burst through the door and walked quickly by her mother. Jordan did not stop to listen to her mother's pleas, but ran out the door and down the street. Barbara Bennett anxiously rubbed her forehead an instant before running after her daughter. By the time Barbara stood on the small porch, Jordan was nearly a block away. Barbara stood dejectedly for a moment before skipping her lunch to drive around the neighborhood looking for her daughter. Her anger turned to anxiety as Jordan was nowhere in sight.

Barbara knew she could not miss work again, so she stopped to ask Brett to look for Jordan after work. The worried mother went back to her job wondering if she would ever understand her daughter.

CHAPTER 6

Jordon crouched behind the corner of the Safeway store as her mother drove slowly looking for her. A part of Jordan was infuriated by her mother's meddling, but another part wanted to hug her mother as she did when she was a child. More than anything now, Jordan wanted to get away. She hid in a long drainage tunnel that ran underneath 14th Street. After her mother's car turned the corner, Jordan climbed out of the culvert and scampered across the busy street. She passed the statue of the Pioneer Woman and ran up the hill toward the mansion.

Jordan had thought of running away from home in the past, but she knew she would eventually go home to face her angry mother. The solitude of the stone mansion on a Saturday afternoon appealed to Jordan today. She looked back over her shoulder to make sure her mother did not follow and entered the mansion grounds.

Jordan veered away from the hotel and snuck past the mansion's public entrance to the open field in the back. There were several smaller stone structures around the rock gate to the west of the big house and the sunlight glistened off the rippling waves of a small, dark lake about two hundred yards from the north entrance. Jordan turned from looking at the lake to admire the large mansion and fantasize what it would be like to live in such a magnificent home.

A stern voice interrupted Jordan's daydream. "What are you doing here?"

Jordan turned to see the odd, old woman she had met a couple of days earlier standing within ten steps of her. The woman wore a tattered lime green raincoat and some kind of flannel pants that almost looked like pajamas. She cuddled her sad-looking cat in her frail arms.

"It's you!" the old woman remarked. "You were spying on me last night."

Jordan replied in a soft voice. "I wasn't spying."

"You were watching me," the old woman charged.

"Yes ma'am," Jordan admitted.

"What was a girl your age doing out that time of night?" the old woman asked.

"I—I followed my brother into the woods," Jordan replied.

"What for?" the woman asked as she looked in the direction of the woods.

"My brother and his friends were looking for golf balls," Jordan confessed.

The old woman looked strangely at Jordan with an almost girlish grin that revealed her nearly toothless smile and said, "They went swimming in the pond by the golf course. I used to love swimming when I was a girl."

Jordan was caught off guard by the woman's sudden amiable demeanor, but she had a hard time imagining the old woman swimming or doing anything else that might be fun. The old woman stiffly bent down to release her cat.

The old woman looked at the silent Jordan before turning to the big house to ask, "You're admiring the palace?"

Jordon took her eyes off the old woman to look at the big house she had been staring at before the old woman interrupted her.

"Yes," Jordan replied. "I think it's the biggest I've ever seen, but I haven't been too many places."

The old woman continued studying the house and said, "It's the biggest house west of the Mississippi—used to be the biggest by far. They called it the Palace on the Prairie."

"You know about this house?" Jordan smiled.

The woman nodded her head vigorously and said, "I know it well."

"The people must have been rich," Jordan observed.

The woman did not respond immediately, but seemed to contemplate Jordan's statement before saying, "I guess so...but they didn't seem so rich."

"J.J. Reynolds told me the house is haunted," Jordan stated.

The old woman turned her attention away from the house and back to Jordan. "The boy you were watching play baseball the other day?"

Jordan nodded and the woman smiled awkwardly.

"Is it haunted?" Jordan finally asked.

The woman looked at the mansion again, as if taking mental notes of all the odd features and answered, "I think it is."

"Really?" Jordan excitedly replied.

The old woman laughed to herself and said, "It's haunted alright. Not with ghosts and goblins like you think, but this place is haunted with memories."

Jordan did not look convinced and replied, "I saw some little devils or goblins or something on the house."

"What?" the woman asked.

Jordan nodded confidently.

"You must show me," the old woman instructed her.

Jordan began to walk around the house to the place where J.J. had shown her the evil-looking carvings. The old woman walked slowly but steadily as Jordan hurried to the spot.

As they arrived, the woman laughed to herself and said, "I guess that does look a little suspicious. Do you know what they're called?"

"The boys told me it was a gargoyle," Jordan answered.

"Do you know why it's called a gargoyle?" the woman quizzed.

Jordan shook her head, as the old woman said, "When it rains really hard, the water comes through the spout and makes a gurgling sound so people called them gargoyles. They're from European castles."

"What are they doing here?" a curious Jordan asked.

"The house was built to look like a palace," the woman explained. "There are many interesting things about this house…if it could only tell its stories."

"Could you tell me some?" Jordan asked.

"I don't know," the woman replied suspiciously.

"Please," Jordan pleaded.

"You're persistent," the woman sighed.

Jordan looked sheepishly at the woman without replying.

The old woman grinned without really smiling and rubbed her red hands together before saying, "The house belonged to a great man. He came here to find fortune, fame, and…a little adventure I suppose."

"Did he?" Jordan coaxed.

"He did and more," the woman continued. "He made a fortune finding oil. He found fame by how he used his wealth. Everything he did was an adventure. He lived large like an actor on a stage. He had a wife—"

"Was she beautiful?" Jordan interrupted.

"Very," the woman assured her. "Their life was like a fairytale. They had everything they ever wanted except children. His wife wanted children more than anything, but of all the things that went well for them, they could not have children."

As the old woman began to walk, she said, "Let's go back around to the other side and I'll show you some things."

Jordan followed as the old woman continued, "Their old house, which was also a mansion, was filled with happiness and hope…and children."

"You said they couldn't have children," Jordan reminded her.

"Oh, but where there's a will, there is a way," the old woman explained. "The wife was very unhappy, but she had a niece and nephew who liked to visit. They were from back east, but they were not so rich…in fact some years had been very hard for their family. The children loved to come here. The Marlands had the big house, plenty of countryside, and adventures for the children. There was even a big ranch south of town that had circuses and shows with cowboys and trick riders. It was a magical place and they all were happy. They were very happy.

"They were so happy in fact, that in time, the couple adopted the children and they came to live permanently. The children developed friends, had parties, and had a grand time. The girl was about twelve years old and her brother a couple of years older."

"I'm twelve," Jordan volunteered.

"I thought you must be," the woman replied, as she looked at the young girl carefully.

Jordan was mesmerized by the old woman's story and nervously waited to see if she would tell more.

The old woman finally said, "It's hard being twelve, isn't it?"

"I don't know," Jordan replied sheepishly, as she walked slowly behind the old woman.

"I think it is," the old woman said.

"It's probably hard for someone like me," Jordan confessed. "But the girl that came to live in the mansion…she must have been like a princess."

The old woman exhaled a grunting laugh and said, "Everyone thought so, but things aren't always like they seem. The girl was often lonely and wondered why her mother had sent her so far away."

"I wish my mother would go away," Jordan fumed.

"That's a terrible thing to say," the old woman scolded.

"Not about my mother," Jordan assured. "She's always trying to run my life, never listens, and just messes up everything."

"Being a mother's not any easier than being twelve, I suppose," the woman noted.

"Maybe," Jordan shrugged. "But I'd like to live in a big house, with all my family…like the girl."

"Be careful what you ask for," the woman replied. "The girl was treated like a princess, but that doesn't mean she was happy."

The old woman continued to walk slowly around the west side of the house with Jordan following.

"This is the Port Cochere," the old woman explained.

"What?" a confused Jordan asked.

The woman giggled in a way that was odd for an old woman and said, "It means 'Coach Entrance' in French. Buckingham Palace and the White House both have them. It was a place for the horse and carriage to come so guests would not have to get out in the weather. It's the main entrance."

"I thought the front porch was the main entrance," Jordan interrupted.

"No," the old woman continued. "This is where all the visitors would enter. Look at the dogs."

Jordan stopped for a moment to see the heads of four dogs carved into the pillars surrounding the impressive oak doors.

"Those were hunting dogs," the old woman explained. "This whole area used to be in the country. There were several small lakes and woods to the east for hunting. There were five small islands in the lake and children would often come here in the summer, before this house was built and swim to the islands. It was an enchanted place then."

"I thought you said the house was haunted?" Jordan asked.

"Haunted with memories," the old woman clarified. "That was before. There would be great fox hunts and horseback riding on these hills and around the lakes. That's why the house was built here."

"You said they had a mansion closer to town and were happy," Jordan said. "Why did they move?"

Jordan could not help but remember her happier days, when her family lived together in Stillwater.

The old woman stared at Jordan for a moment without saying anything. She looked as if memories from the past were running through her head.

Finally the old woman answered, "The house was built by a great man and great men want to do great things. This house was his dream. It is a place of rare beauty and artistic integrity. It was an expression from his mind into substance, of the quality, the strength, and the heart of the man."

The old woman did not say more and began walking slowly and deliberately away from the entrance. Jordan instinctively followed her, wanting to know more of the story.

"Up there," Jordan pointed. "What does that 'M' and '1927' mean?"

Jordon was asking about a greenish, metal object on the top of the wall of the house that looked like some kind of drain spout.

The old woman stopped walking and without looking said, "The 'M' stands for Marland and 1927 was when the mansion was completed."

"Who's Marland?" Jordan asked.

The woman looked at the young girl in quizzical surprise and asked, "You live in Ponca City and don't know who E.W. Marland is?"

Jordan shook her head.

"What do they teach you in school, if you don't know about E.W. Marland?" the old woman scolded.

"I haven't lived here very long," Jordan meekly replied.

The old woman looked at the timid girl and said in a more compassionate voice, "Yes, I forgot. You told me that. Let me tell you about E.W. Marland, then. He came to Oklahoma with great dreams and exceeded all of them. At his house downtown, he threw grand parties. He had a wonderful, manicured garden...nearly eight acres in all. His oil company grew and there seemed nothing he couldn't do."

"Did the girl go to the parties?" Jordan asked. "The twelve-year-old girl you told me about?"

"When she was older," the woman answered. "Such parties you could hardly imagine. Young men would come from all over just for the chance to dance with her."

"Did she fall in love?" Jordan quizzed.

The old woman looked away from Jordan for a moment to stare at the mansion before saying, "She did...once. Her life was complicated. The parties were grand just the same."

Jordan had many questions about the mansion and the young woman who had lived in it, but before she could ask, the old woman became distracted and agitated.

"There he is again," the old woman fumed.

Jordan turned around to see the man who had followed her the previous afternoon.

"Who is he?" Jordan asked with a hint of disdain in her voice.

The question was unanswered, as Jordon turned around to see the old woman walking quickly in the opposite direction toward one of the stone buildings on the edge of the mansion property. The old woman's cat raised her back at the intruder before trotting after the old woman. Jordan looked back to see the man walking forcefully toward her. Jordan turned to see where the old woman was going and was surprised to see she had vanished. Jordan had a strange feeling about this mysterious woman who continually disappeared on a whim. Jordan did not have time to think about that, as she watched the man walk directly toward her.

Jordan wanted to run, but did not know where she could go. The property seemed to be vacant except for her and the odd man approaching her. The man moved toward her carrying a polished black walking stick. The man had a peculiar tilt to his dark hat. Jordan's heart sank as the man came close enough for her to see it was Mr. Grumman from the corner house on her street.

As Jordan gained her wits enough to begin walking away, a forceful male voice yelled, "Stop!"

A frightened Jordan wanted to run, but the man shouted again in a more compelling voice, "Please!"

Jordan turned to face the man who continued steadily toward her. Mr. Grumman was dressed in a business suit, although it was Saturday and very warm. He walked with a bowlegged waddle that made him look almost comical.

"Young woman," the man panted as he approached. "Please, wait a moment."

Jordan felt compelled to obey the old man who was now only twenty or so steps away, although she had been coached by everyone to keep her distance from Mr. Grumman.

"Were you talking to Lydie?" Mr. Grumman asked.

"Who's Lydie?" Jordan asked.

"Lydie Marland," the old man replied with a raised eyebrow. "The woman you were talking to."

Jordan looked around, but did not see the old woman. She had never asked the woman her name, but assumed this man must have known her.

"I was just talking to her," Jordan shared. "I didn't know her name."

"She's very particular about who she talks to," the man explained.

"Did she happen to say anything about a statue?" the man asked.

"No," Jordan said.

The man looked at her carefully and asked, "Nothing at all?"

"No," Jordan assured him.

"Think carefully," the old man suggested. "It's very important."

Jordan looked at the eager, old man and said, "I don't really know what you're talking about."

The man seemed disappointed and asked pointedly, "What did you and Lydie talk about?"

Jordan looked at the old man strangely and said, "Not really anything...she talked about this house and some parties. She's—"

"Suspicious," the old man interrupted.

"Yes," Jordan replied quickly, as that was the exact word she would have used to describe the old woman.

"She's been that way for years," the old man added.

"So you know her?" Jordan asked.

The old man nodded and said, "For many years."

A confused Jordan asked, "Why don't you ask her then?"

The old man laughed insincerely and said, "I have, but she won't tell. I think she's the only one who knows where it is. She seems to have taken a liking to you. I thought maybe she had said something about it."

"About what?" Jordan asked.

The old man rubbed the back of his neck and said, "There's a statue. It's very valuable and I would like to find it. I think it's buried somewhere close, but she won't tell."

"Jordan!" a voice yelled from the distance.

Jordan looked up to see her brother, Brett running toward her.

"Is that your brother?" Mr. Grumman asked.

Jordan nodded.

With a scowl, the old man looked at the boy running toward them and said, "I wouldn't ask her about the statue. Like you've seen, Lydie's very...secretive. And tell your brother to stay away from my house."

The old man hurriedly walked away as Brett ran up to Jordan.

"Was that Mr. Grumpy?" a concerned Brett asked.

Jordan nodded.

"What did he want?" Brett quizzed.

"I don't know," Jordan replied. "He asked about some old statue and...he said something about you staying away from his house."

"Like I'd hang out at Grumpy Old Man's Corner," Brett fumed. "Where have you been?"

"Here," Jordan replied.

"You're in big trouble," Brett said. "I've never seen Mom so mad."

"I know," Jordan sighed.

"Why can't you give Mom a break?" Brett asked.

Jordan thought for a moment and replied, "I don't know."

Brett looked at his sister carefully. It had been a hard year for their family, but it seemed to be much harder on his sister than anyone else. He did not exactly understand why, but he did feel sorry for her.

"We better get home before Mom," Brett suggested. "I'll tell her you came right back...Maybe I can save your life."

Jordan nodded obediently. Brett nudged her arm and the two siblings walked slowly away from the mansion. As Jordan passed the iron gate, she looked back to admire the majestic mansion in the afternoon sun. Looking through the Port Cochere, Jordan could see the old woman standing in the distance in the shade watching her. Jordan wanted to go and talk to her, but she felt the old woman would simply disappear again. She had tried her brother's patience enough for one day, so she followed him dutifully down the hill to their modest house. Jordan dreaded facing her mother, but knew her hour of reckoning was near.

CHAPTER 7

Jordan entered her house followed by Brett. She felt guilty about the mess she had left in the front room. Although Jordan was still angry with her mother, she understood why her mother had been disappointed earlier. In near panic, Jordan hurriedly began straightening up the room. She did not ask, but Brett feverishly helped her. The brother and sister had only made minor progress when the screen door creaked open. Jordan looked at her brother an instant before her mother entered the house.

Barbara Bennett looked stoically at the half-cleaned room before fixing her gaze on Jordan. Without a word, Barbara stepped quickly toward her daughter and squeezed her tightly.

In a quivering tone, Barbara said, "I was so worried about you."

Jordan cried and she surprised herself by saying, "I'm sorry."

Brett stood by awkwardly, as his sister and mother sobbed together in the front room.

"You're still grounded," Barbara finally said.

"I know," Jordan replied.

Her mother's tearful hug tamed Jordan's earlier anger. The young girl still resented her mother's indifference to the feelings she held toward her father, but for some reason, being hugged on a Saturday afternoon comforted Jordan.

As chaotic as life had been at the Bennett home the past year, the one constant Barbara had been able to maintain was her family's church attendance. On Sunday, she would drive the children a few blocks to a church on Hartford Avenue, north of their home. Jordan usually paid little attention to the short drive, but today she peered curiously up the hill toward the Marland Mansion hoping to catch a glimpse of the odd, old woman she talked to the day before. She could see no sign of the woman, however, and settled in the backseat.

Jordan had mixed feelings about the family's Sunday ritual. She did not mind the actual service, but hated being around families that were not torn apart like hers. Although other mothers brought their children to church while husbands stayed behind, Jordan felt as if church people did not know how to deal with her family's broken home. The church had an energetic youth minister that taught the high school class, but Jordan's junior high class had a middle-aged deacon reading a lesson straight from his quarterly Bible material. There were several kids she recognized from school, but Linda Pelletier was the only girl she remotely knew. Linda was a plain, shy girl that sometimes ate lunch with Jordan at school. The girl was average height with straight brown hair and pale skin.

Linda was thin, like Jordan, and she wore bulky-looking braces on her teeth. Jordan liked Linda well enough, but always felt as if their shared awkwardness was their only true bond.

"Heard you got grounded," a pleasant voice greeted Jordan as she moved from class to the auditorium for worship services.

A smiling Brad Cooper grinned at her. Jordan nodded politely as she headed to her pew to sit with the other young people. She did not feel particularly comfortable with the youth group, but it was better than the humiliation of sitting with her mother. Jordan never thought about her mother's weekly burden of sitting alone in a nearly full auditorium.

Sunday after church offered some true peace in the house. Barbara Bennett usually had a small roast in the oven, with carrots and potatoes baked with it. She would spend a little time cleaning the house for the upcoming week and then retreat to her room to read a magazine or take a nap. Jordan enjoyed being alone in her room while she dreaded the upcoming school week.

About two o'clock, an angry knock ended Jordan's afternoon nap. She heard voices at the front door and moved to the hallway to see what was happening. Jordan froze when she recognized the voice of Mr. Grumman, who lived on the corner. Jordan stayed out of sight, but listened as her mother apologized and shut the door.

"Brett!" Barbara Bennett shouted in a tone normally reserved for Jordan. "Brett!"

"I think he went outside," Jordan finally interrupted. "Is everything okay?"

"Mr. Grumman thinks Brett has been prowling around his house," Barbara Bennett explained.

"Brett wouldn't do that," Jordan protested. "You've always told us to stay away from that place."

"I know," Barbara replied. "Mr. Grumman thinks that every boy in this neighborhood lives in this house."

The Bennett house had been the hangout for many of Brett's friends during the summer.

"It was probably J.J. Reynolds or one of his little— friends," Barbara concluded. "Mr. Grumman was agitated nonetheless. I thought he was going to have a stroke."

Barbara Bennett continued with her cleaning and Jordan retreated back to her room without giving Mr. Grumman another thought.

For the next two weeks, Jordan came home after school to an empty house, with explicit orders not to leave the confines of the yard. She was tempted to sneak off a few afternoons, just to defy her mother, but decided to do her time and stay at the house.

Her brother Brett always knew how to take care of his sister and he stayed around the house, although his friends begged him to come to the field and play football. Brett made some feeble excuses, but Jordan felt warm inside knowing her brother was committed to staying with her. Jordan never considered he might be staying around the house to keep her from getting into even more trouble, which ultimately would cause him more grief.

After the first day, Brad Cooper came to hang out with Brett and the next day J.J. Reynolds stopped by the house.

After that, the whole gang of boys came to the Bennett house each afternoon. Jordan believed the boys were there to cheer her up and even imagined that J.J. Reynolds secretly liked teasing her by calling her "JorDAN." It never occurred to her that the boys had discovered that Brett had a house void of adult supervision. All Jordan knew was that she was not alone. She got to hang out with the boys and enjoyed being the only girl in their group.

One evening, Barbara Bennett pulled into the driveway and as usual, Brett's friends began to scatter.

"Hold on!" Barbara Bennett shouted as the boys headed away from the house. "Who did it?"

"Who did what?" Brett asked.

"Someone vandalized Mr. Grumman's fence and now he's in the hospital," Barbara explained. "I knew he was upset Sunday, but I didn't think he would literally make himself sick."

"We didn't do anything," Brett replied.

"How about you, J.J.?" Barbara accused, as she cut her eyes toward the young man who was slowly trying to get out of sight.

"I don't know anything," J.J. claimed. "Everyone knows the old man is a freak and we've always been told to stay away from the house."

"He's not a freak," Barbara asserted. "He's a bit odd, but we're all a little odd sometimes. Are you sure you didn't do anything to his fence?"

"No ma'am," J.J. said, shaking his head.

Mrs. Bennett looked at the other boys and none claimed responsibility.

"You boys leave that old man alone," Barbara threatened. "He'll call the police next time."

"Is he okay?" Brett asked.

"Yes," Barbara affirmed. "I saw him today when I did my clinical at the hospital. He'll recover and be home in a few days. You boys need to go home now."

As his friends left, Barbara Bennett turned to her son and asked, "Do you want to tell me the truth now?"

Jordan was not accustomed to seeing her older brother even close to trouble so she anxiously listened for him to answer.

Brett stared at his feet for a minute before saying, "It was J.J., but he didn't vandalize anything. Some of the guys were telling stories about Mr. Grumpy—I mean Mr. Grumman. They thought he had some weird stuff in his backyard, so they dared J.J. to take a look."

"What kind of 'weird stuff' did they think they would see?" Barbara asked.

"I don't know," Brett replied. "Really, I don't know. It was just guys talking."

Barbara did not press the issue, but asked, "What did J.J. do?"

Brett sighed heavily and said, "He went down there and knocked some knot holes out of the fence to look inside."

"What did he see?" Barbara asked.

"Not much," Brett answered. "J.J. said there was a small patio with some furniture and a backyard. There were some stones, but J.J. said he didn't get a good look."

"I hope you boys are proud of yourselves," Barbara scolded. "You're lucky Mr. Grumman didn't have a heart attack."

"I'm sorry," Brett admitted.

"There's about an hour of sunlight left," Barbara observed. "I want you to get the lawnmower and mow Mr. Grumman's front yard. Stay out of the back, but I don't want him to have to mow in this heat when he gets out of the hospital."

"Why me?" Brett protested. "I didn't do anything."

"You weren't completely truthful with me, were you?" Barbara noted.

"No, ma'am," Brett acknowledged. "I'll get on it."

Barbara patted her son on the shoulder before going inside.

"Jordan," Barbara said, "Come help with supper."

Jordan was less than thrilled at having to cook supper, but she was happy to not be the one in trouble for a change. She helped her mother and avoided any sharp comments or confrontations. The temporary peace was broken when Brett burst through the door and startled them.

"What is it?" a concerned Barbara asked.

"I don't know what happened," Brett replied.

"Are you okay?" Barbara said, as she examined her son.

"It's the lawnmower," Brett said. "I don't know what happened. I messed up."

Barbara Bennett, relieved that her son was not hurt, asked, "What?"

"I'll have to show you," Brett sighed.

Brett headed out the door with his mother following and Jordan tagging behind. At the corner, Jordan could audibly hear her mother gasp as she looked at the yard.

"What happened?" Barbara Bennett said, nearly in tears.

"I don't know," Brett tried to explain. "I thought I checked things, but something happened to the mower. I made four passes before I noticed."

Jordan looked at Mr. Grumman's yard which had four uneven scalp strips across the otherwise green yard. One set of wheels had obviously been set too low, mangling the lawn where Brett had mowed.

"This won't grow back before Mr. Grumman comes home," Barbara moaned. "It may not grow back before winter."

Frantically Barbara looked around the empty street.

"Did anyone see you?" Barbara anxiously asked.

"I don't know," Brett answered.

"Quick," Barbara instructed. "Push the mower into our backyard."

Brett obeyed his mother and hurriedly pushed the worn-out mower while his mother surveyed the neighborhood to see if they could get back home without being seen. Barbara ushered Jordan into the house and Brett soon joined them. The trio stood silently, as if someone might hear their conversation through the walls.

"You can't tell anyone," Barbara finally instructed in a hushed voice.

Brett nodded while Jordan smirked.

"What are you grinning about?" a frenzied Barbara asked her daughter.

"Don't you think it's funny?" Jordan asked.

"No!" Barbara replied. "What could be funny about ruining Mr. Grumman's yard?"

"You punished Brett for being less than truthful," Jordan explained. "Now you want us to lie."

A stern Barbara Bennett stared at her daughter before saying, "Well—sometimes we need to camouflage the truth a little."

Brett and Jordan looked at each other and then at their mother.

Barbara Bennett sighed heavily and said, "Poor Mr. Grumman will think someone vandalized him for sure now."

Barbara looked at her children and began to smile. She had not smiled much the past months, but the absurdity of the situation now dawned on her. Brett was the first to laugh, followed by Jordan. Barbara soon joined her children chuckling enthusiastically in the privacy of their small home. Barbara laughed until she nearly cried.

"This will be our little secret," Barbara finally declared. "Mr. Grumman doesn't need to know that we're the vandals in the neighborhood."

Barbara stepped to the window to look outside and continued, "Let's hope it's a secret to everyone else, too."

The family laughed about Brett's mistake a few minutes more, which caused Barbara to grin playfully. Her smile, however, faded to a frown as she returned to her room and remembered the more ominous secret she was keeping from her children.

CHAPTER 8

Jordan tolerated school. She did not have many acquaintances, much less friends, at the junior high. Lunch periods became particularly intimidating. Every day she feared having to sit at a table alone, or worse, having the wrong kids sit with her. Today she was at the front of the lunch line and was faced with a number of vacant tables. She chose one in the corner of the cafeteria and watched out the corner of her eye as person after person avoided her. When Linda Pelletier showed up in the lunch room, Jordan held her breath hoping the quiet girl would join her.

"Hey, Jordan," Linda meekly greeted her, as she took a seat.

"Hi, Linda," a relieved Jordan replied.

Linda plopped down beside Jordan and picked at the tacos in front of her. Jordan knew Linda from church, and the quiet girl was about as close as she had to a friend at school.

With a heavy sigh, Linda said, "I guess this technically qualifies as food."

Jordan smiled at the assessment and nodded. Linda picked through her plate and did not eat much of the food she had criticized.

"Did you get your math homework done?" Linda asked.

"I'm going to the library after lunch and finish it," Jordan answered.

"Cool," Linda shrugged.

"How about you?" Jordan asked, trying to maintain the conversation.

"Sure," Linda answered. "I have no life."

There was nothing about Linda Pelletier that suggested humor. She had straight brown hair that she often wore in a stringy ponytail. Her grayish-brown eyes seemed devoid of life, but she had a dry, cutting wit that matched Jordan's sometimes cynical view of school life.

"Do you want some help with the math?" Linda offered.

"Naw," Jordan shook her head. "I've got it—thanks, though."

"No problem," Linda stated. "We 'get-alongers' have got to stick together."

"Huh?" a confused Jordan grunted.

Linda looked around the lunchroom and explained, "We're surrounded by punks and jocks, band guys, the brainiacs, the hoods, the smokers…we're get-alongers. We survive this place by getting along."

Jordan laughed and nodded at Linda's observation. The social complexities of junior high often seemed daunting to Jordan and she felt some satisfaction knowing her feelings of inadequacy were shared by someone.

"That's how I survive," Jordan agreed. "I've learned to get along with all the groups."

"Teachers have their groups too," Linda continued. "The meanies, the cool teachers, the easy teachers, the strict teachers, the hard teachers. Don't think they don't know what they're doing. They probably all go to the teacher's lounge before the school year starts to decide who's going to be what."

"You've got it all figured out," Jordan noted.

"I've lived here longer than you," Linda shrugged. "What'cha doing this weekend?"

It was only Thursday and Jordan had not thought about the weekend at all, but she knew the answer as she replied, "Nothing—I'm still grounded."

"Bummer," Linda replied. "I'm going to the game Saturday. We got an extra ticket and I thought you might want to come."

"Game?" Jordan asked.

"The Oklahoma State game," Linda clarified. "It's just Illinois State, but we might win."

"In Stillwater?" Jordan quizzed.

"Yeah," Linda nodded. "We play at Nebraska next week and this will be the last home game for a while."

"I'd like to," Jordan sighed, "but—I'm still grounded. My mom's a real killjoy about anything fun."

"But you could ask," Linda smiled.

Jordan nodded. She finished her lunch and hurried to the library to do her math assignment due that afternoon. Jordan was not sure she would bother asking her mother if she could go to the game, but she appreciated Linda eating lunch with her. She needed a friend, and Linda was at least trying to take the job.

CHAPTER 9

After school, Jordan endured another bus ride before slowly walking up 13th Street to her empty house. She looked forward to a few moments alone before Brett arrived. As she stepped on the front porch, Jordan heard a strange, muffled sound she could not identify. She listened for a few seconds, but did not hear the sound again.

Jordan glanced at the corner house to see a perturbed Mr. Grumman looking at his strangely striped front lawn. Jordan stared too long. As Mr. Grumman looked up to glare meanly at her, Jordan scampered inside and peered out the window to see the scowling Mr. Grumman watching her house.

Jordan heard Brett arrive with a couple of his friends and Mr. Grumman retreated to his house. Brett rushed inside to retrieve a basketball without bothering his sister. Jordan stayed inside, but she could hear several more boys in the driveway telling stories and shooting baskets.

Jordan watched a rerun of *Star Trek*, but soon noticed something strange—silence from the front yard. She looked outside to see the boys quietly huddled by the corner of the house. As she crept outside, all the boys looked intently at the ground.

"What's going on?" she asked softly.

Jordan felt compelled to whisper, although she had no idea why she needed to talk in hushed tones.

"Do you hear it?" Brad Cooper whispered back.

Jordan listened for a few seconds before saying, "I don't hear anything."

Her answer was greeted with a host of hissing, "Shhhhh!"

Jordan was about to respond when she heard a faint, scratching sound.

"I heard it!" several boys declared in unison.

Jordan listened carefully to the same strange, faint sound she thought she had heard earlier.

"I'm telling you," J.J. Reynolds declared, "this house is haunted."

"Shut-up, J.J.," Brett demanded. "You think every house is haunted and we don't want to hear another story. It's coming from the ground."

"Where do you think the dead are?" J.J. responded.

"It's coming from the drain pipe," Brad Cooper declared.

At the corner of the house, the gutter from the roof emptied into a pipe that went into the ground and took the water to the street. Jordan remembered the story the old woman had told her about the gargoyles and the gurgling sound they made after a rain.

"It's probably just water running," Jordan observed.

Brett considered his sister's idea a moment before saying, "It hasn't rained in weeks."

Jordon had not thought about that.

"Something's down there!" J.J. announced. "I saw it, I swear."

The rest of the group was dubious, but Brett looked down the small dark hole and said, "He's right."

The boys crowded around the small hole to look for themselves.

"What is it?" Brad Cooper asked.

Brett looked down the dark hole and then up the drain pipe to the guttering before saying, "It must be a bird."

The boys all agreed and seemed content to have solved the mystery when a panicked Jordan said, "We've got to get her out!"

The boys all looked at each other for a moment before nodding in agreement, although none of them seemed to have a plan to rescue the poor creature. Brett finally went into the house to retrieve some tools. In a moment, he separated the guttering from the drain that led to the street. Down the dark hole the boys could see something struggling.

"You've got to do something," Jordan pleaded.

"Yeah," J.J. added. "Reach in and get it."

"I'm not getting pecked," Brett responded.

Brett looked up at the guttering and back at the drain. He then walked down the short driveway.

"The drain leads to the street," Brett reasoned, talking almost to himself. "If we put water down the drain, it should flush the bird out the other end."

The boys may not have been convinced the plan would work, but none of them wanted to reach into the dark hole and grab the animal. Brett fetched the garden hose from the side of the house and prepared to flush the drain with water. About half the boys went to the street to see the exit point and the rest stayed with Brett as he began putting water down the drain. There was hushed silence for a few seconds, as the rescue captivated the boys' full attention. In a moment however, the drain began to back up and water flooded up the drain and into the driveway. Before Brett could shut the water off, a collective group scream erupted as an angry wet squirrel hustled out of the hole looking like a drowned rat.

The squirrel scampered around in dazed confusion as the boys shrieked—rushing into the house in an instant. Jordan stood alone in the driveway, as all the boys peered out from behind the safety of the screen door. The exhausted squirrel was pathetic as he stared at Jordan before trotting off to the safety of the neighbor's backyard. The boys slowly came out of the house, keeping a wary eye out for the angry squirrel.

In a few moments, the boys forgot their cowardice and began laughing at the incident. They imagined what the poor squirrel must have been thinking and after a while began congratulating themselves for the rescue of the poor animal. Jordan quietly watched the boys tease each other when she looked down the street to see Mr. Grumman standing on his porch glaring at them. When Mr. Grumman saw Jordan watching him, he retreated into his house. Jordan did not know what to think of the strange man, but something about him caused her to feel uneasy.

Jordan went back inside after a few minutes of watching the boys and felt a strange sense of satisfaction in knowing the squirrel was safe. She did not bother to tease the boys about how they screamed like little girls when the squirrel sprinted out of its hole. Jordan believed she could empathize with the poor squirrel as she too had often felt trapped with no way out. The great squirrel rescue became part of the neighborhood lore, but it marked an end of childhood for the group in some ways. The boys still played their sports in the ever shortening afternoons, but high school slowly but surely placed them in groups that tested their previous camaraderie.

Jordan sat alone in the house while the boys reveled in the fading days of their boyhood. She had made one friend at school, although her interaction with Linda Pelletier only included brief conversations a couple of days each week at lunch. Her relationship with Linda, however, only reminded her of how much she missed her best friend Chloe from her home in Stillwater. Chloe had been the closest thing to a sister she had ever known, and Jordan desperately wanted to see her. Without her friend, Jordan felt as trapped and desperate as the poor wet squirrel they had freed.

CHAPTER 10

By October, a liberated Jordan left the house after weeks of being grounded. Her good behavior caused a temporary improvement in the relationship with her mother. Pretending to be obedient created an illusion of tranquility in the family. The crisp, pleasant autumn air meant shorter days. Jordan headed quickly toward the Marland Mansion. She had not seen Lydie in weeks and was curious to discover what mysteries the old woman might reveal.

The bleached-brown grass of the season blended with the stately stone walls of the mansion, with only a few ornamental plants showing contrasting colors. The middle of the week meant few cars around the hotel to the south of the mansion. The thick trees beyond the hotel were also turning brown and Jordan noticed she could see further down the path leading into the wooded area. Jordan walked lazily around the eastside of the mansion and stopped on the north terrace for a moment to daydream.

A quick rush of a cat pouncing on some imaginary prey startled Jordan for an instant.

Jordan watched the cat for a second before kneeling down and coaxing, "Come here, kitty. I won't hurt you."

Jordan knelt down and reached out her hand, but the stubborn cat stared at her before stretching its back and strolling away.

"It's you again," a voice interrupted from behind.

Jordan looked up to see the old woman she had met a few weeks earlier.

"What are you doing here?" the old woman questioned as she walked closer.

"I—I'm just looking," Jordan responded. "I was trying to make friends with your cat."

The old woman kept walking and soon hunched over the crouching young girl.

"That cat is picky in choosing her friends," the woman explained.

"What's her name?" Jordan asked.

The woman at first looked perturbed at the question, but then answered, "She's just a cat. I think they called her Florence because she was part of a litter of cats that someone named after great cities. There was Cairo, Sydney, Chicago, Dallas, and Florence. Florence is a great name for a city, but not much of a name for a cat. She doesn't respond to any name so I don't call her anything."

"I like looking at the house," Jordan said, changing the subject. "I've been trying to imagine the parties you told me about."

In a more pleasant tone of voice, the old woman said, "I like to come and look at the old house myself sometimes."

Jordan stood in awkward silence for a moment before saying, "You're the girl, aren't you?"

"What?" the old woman asked suspiciously.

"Last time I saw you," Jordan explained, "you told me about the Marlands and the young girl that came to live with them. You are the girl!"

The woman stared coldly at Jordan and sternly asked, "How would you know that?"

Jordan looked nervously at the old woman and timidly answered, "A man—told me."

"What man?" the woman demanded.

Jordan thought intently for a moment and answered, "Mr. Grumman."

"Teddy Grumman?" the woman whispered to herself with a slight tone of disdain.

"I don't know his first name," Jordan replied. "He said—he said he was a friend of yours."

The old woman looked sternly at the young girl, as if trying to read her thoughts and finally replied, "I suppose that's true, but that was many years ago and a lot has happened since those days. What did he want?"

Jordan thought back to the conversation and said, "He asked what we talked about. He asked about you, if you were okay and things like that."

"Always spying on me like all the others," the old woman muttered.

"He said," Jordan began, before stopping to think.

In a more deliberate tone, Jordan continued, "He said you were the girl. He said you were Lydie Marland."

The old woman looked away from Jordan and gazed at the mansion, as if searching for some memory that had been lost long ago.

"Teddy Grumman's never been a liar," the old woman sighed. "He told you the truth, but he shouldn't have."

Jordan could do nothing but look at the woman for a moment before finally asking, "What was it like? I mean, what was it like to live in the mansion? You said it was like being a princess."

The old woman's forehead wrinkled as she said, "It was so long ago...like it never happened. I don't like to think about it."

"I think I understand," Jordan replied.

The old woman looked quizzically at the young girl and said, "Really?"

"Yeah," Jordan explained. "It's not easy being twelve."

The old woman laughed strangely and asked, "Why? Why did you say it's not easy being twelve?"

"You said that's how old you were when you came to live here," Jordan replied.

The old woman shook her head and said, "It can be difficult being twelve, but for me this place was like a paradise. The weather was warm; I had ponies and friends. It was one of the best times of my life."

"So," Jordan coaxed. "What was it like in the mansion?"

The old woman looked around nervously and said, "You are persistent. It was…It was like a dream, I suppose. None of it seemed real…it still doesn't seem real to me. There were parties and games. My brother and I used to put on these plays, we would have playbills printed, make costumes, and put on the production for the neighbors. It was great fun and I think some of our plays were quite amusing. Besides the parties and the plays, there were fox hunts and traveling. It was an enchanted life."

Lydie stopped to look at Jordan and surveyed their lonely surroundings before asking, "Would you like to see inside?"

A surprised Jordan replied, "Sure, but isn't it closed for the afternoon?"

"I can get you in," Lydie assured her.

As Jordan took a step toward the entrance, the old woman said, "Not that way."

Lydie walked away from the house toward a structure built into the side of a small hill. The building overlooked a field where the boys often played. The unusual edifice looked like the underneath side of a bridge with a walkway above and three distinctive arches sheltering a stone patio. The woman headed underneath the arches and looked around anxiously.

"What is this place?" Jordan asked.

The old woman replied, "The boathouse."

Jordan looked around skeptically at the grassy lawn stretching out from the arches with nothing but a small pond almost one hundred yards away.

"There used to be a lake here years ago," the old woman explained. "It dried up and they filled it in. They used to store the boats in this place."

"Why are we here?" Jordan asked.

The woman tried to restrain her smile and said, "You'll see."

The old woman faced a massive wood door made of sturdy wooden planks, which gave it a fortified appearance and continued, "They don't know I have a key."

Lydie held an antique-looking key and slowly fit it into the lock and jiggled it furiously.

"Help me," she asked.

Jordon stepped in front of the woman and pulled on the heavy door. She was surprised when with an ominous squeak, it moved. The door opened to a long dark room with a stale dankness to the air.

"Scat," the old woman instructed her cat. "You can't come in here."

Jordan looked at the dark room while the cat glanced inside before strolling back toward the sunshine.

"Come," the old woman coaxed, as she disappeared into the darkness.

Jordan did not know what to do, when the old woman vanished in the gloomy, blackness.

"Come on," Lydie repeated and Jordan stepped into the dark room.

Jordan had never been in a place so black. She could not see Lydie and could not even see the walls of the room. Jordon let out an astonished gasp when the old woman produced a small, pocket flashlight. Jordan could not believe what she was seeing. What she thought to be a long dark room was actually a curving tunnel heading into the earth. The tunnel was about ten feet across and wide enough for the two of them to walk side-by-side. The arching ceiling was smooth and the concrete floor appeared to be completely covered in dampness and occasional puddles of water.

"Follow me," the old woman commanded, as she walked into the long tunnel.

A frightened but curious Jordan stepped into the tunnel to follow the woman. Jordon listened to the click-clack of their steps and felt her shoes splattering a thin film of black water as she walked in the shadowy darkness. The light from outside faded as they followed the curving tunnel.

"Where—" Jordan began to ask, as a strong echo bounced off an unseen wall and the woman pointed at her to be quiet.

Jordan continued to follow, but the echo made their steps on the wet concrete reverberate unnaturally. They walked in the darkness nearly two hundred yards. Suddenly Lydie stopped and the dim flashlight made the woman's wrinkled skin glow frightfully, showing the creases and anguish in her face that indicated a long, hard life.

"We're here," Lydie whispered softly.

Jordan believed she could hear the echoes of the old woman's heavy breathing in the tunnel. Lydie pushed open another heavy door with a heavy sigh and Jordan felt warm, fresh air in the dark space in front of them. The old woman walked easily through the small room with the aid of her flashlight and in a few seconds turned on a light switch illuminating a naked light bulb in a sparsely furnished room about twelve feet square.

"What is this place?" Jordan asked.

"You must talk softly," the old woman instructed.

Jordan nodded indicating her understanding.

"We're in the house now," the woman said softly. "This is where the men used to play poker and where the bootleggers brought the—party supplies. There's another room up there that Mr. Marland once used to use to hide his liquor, but they haven't found that yet. Come on."

The small room looked utilitarian and cluttered. The old woman stopped a moment and moved some items for no apparent reason. Jordan followed the woman through a door into a large kitchen that opened into a larger room with a high ceiling and pictures painted on the beams.

"It's huge," Jordan gasped.

"This is where they used to have parties for the fox hunts," the woman explained. "The pictures on the ceiling tell the history of this property."

"Wow!" Jordan replied, as she looked at the colorful paintings.

"Shhh!" the woman signaled with her hand to her mouth.

Jordan froze and soon heard the rhythmic clicking of shoes on the hard floor. The woman motioned Jordan to follow her toward the end of the room dominated by a huge fireplace. The stone fireplace was big enough for Jordan to stand in and the woman walked right to it, before pulling a paneled door open. The two entered the dark space and listened to the steps come closer before they became silent when a distant door creaked open and shut. The room where they hid was the size of a small cellar with no windows and only the hidden paneled entrance.

"What was that?" Jordan asked.

"The security guard, Russell," the woman explained. "He walks through pretty often, but he makes so much noise he never sees me. There are plenty of places to hide in this house."

"Will we get in trouble?" Jordan asked.

"No," the woman replied. "This is my house, after all."

In a few minutes, the woman peeked out of the hidden space before walking across the tile floor and down a long hall with eerie carvings of fat men with strange expressions on their faces. Jordan noticed the old woman wore rubber-soled tennis shoes. The woman walked more quickly than Jordan would have thought and she moved with an unmistakable grace.

Jordan had never been inside the mansion and marveled at the many carvings. The ceilings and floors were ornate. Although the large spaces were sparsely furnished and empty, Jordan could easily imagine the parties the old woman had described. Jordan's tour guide moved quickly and silently through the house. Strange echoes reverberated with the slightest sound and Jordan noticed the old woman would occasionally pick up and move items for no reason.

"This way," Lydie instructed.

The woman entered a small door that led through another large kitchen area and then to a maintenance space. An old room with two beds occupied the corner of the basement.

"Do you live here?" Jordan asked.

"No," the woman assured her. "This used to be the maid's quarters, but I think the security guards use it for naps these days."

The old woman opened another plain door revealing a staircase. Jordan followed as the woman moved slowly but steadily up narrow stairs. After about forty steps, she cautiously opened a door to peer out before motioning for Jordan to step into a magnificent large ballroom.

Jordan admired a glossily-polished black and white checkered patterned floor in an impressive room that could accommodate several hundred people. A long, open walkway connected the large area with another even larger room at the end. Jordan was marveling at the ornate, gold leaf ceiling when something on the wall caught her attention. Another large fireplace adorned the room, but the architecture of the room was not what interested young Jordan.

"That's you!" Jordan excitedly whispered as she looked at a large painting of a beautiful young woman in an elegant, flowing white gown.

The old woman stood by Jordan and looked at the painting for a moment before saying, "I suppose it is. I never much liked that painting, however."

"It's beautiful," Jordan admired. "You were beautiful."

The old woman giggled to herself and replied, "I think you emphasized 'were' a little too much. I don't hardly remember the girl in the picture any longer...I do remember the times."

"How can that be?" Jordan asked. "It's you."

"It was a long, long time ago," the old woman whispered, as she walked away.

Lydie did not want to talk about the painting so Jordan patiently followed her as she quietly continued the tour of the great mansion. Jordan marveled at the ornate rooms, polished floors, and intricate carvings. Lydie stopped in a small yellow room.

The old woman stood silently for a moment, before saying, "This was Mr. Marland's favorite room."

"Here?" Jordan questioned, as she scanned the plain room.

The old woman nodded and said, "He liked to look out the window. You could see the lake back in the old days."

Jordan looked out the window to see the boathouse and the entrance to the secret tunnel.

"Don't you worry about getting in trouble, sneaking in like this?" Jordan asked.

The woman shook her head and said, "I know this place like the back of my own hand. I was here when they were building it. I know every hiding place and I know how to be discreet—I know every secret of this place. Besides, what are they going to do but throw me out?"

"Why don't you live here?" Jordan innocently asked.

"That's a long story," the old woman explained. "This place is very big and would be lonely, I suspect. I'm happy just to see the city is taking care of things. It makes me happy to know people come here to visit."

Lydie stopped talking abruptly and listened to a muffled sound coming from inside the large house. In a moment, a security guard whistling cheerfully indicated his approach.

"Follow me," she said urgently.

The old woman stepped quickly to a nondescript door and stepped back to the secret stairway. Instead of going down, she headed up the steps and soon came to a small room filled with years of clutter.

"What's this place?" Jordan asked.

"The sewing room," the old woman explained. "A seamstress once worked here. Behind this room is the cedar room."

Jordan stepped past the woman to look into a small room with the distinctive aroma of cedar. The room was completely covered in cedar paneling with shelves and drawers built into the walls.

"This is where the seasonal clothes were stored," the woman explained. "The stairs lead to the bedrooms upstairs and above this room is the trunk room where the luggage was stored. You can take the stairs from the basement to the attic and few people know it's even here."

The old woman showed Jordan several vacant bedrooms. The largest room featured rich wood paneling and connected to another room with delicate carvings on the walls and ceilings. A dainty marble fireplace caused the old woman to stare strangely at the nearly empty room.

"This was your room, wasn't it?" Jordan asked.

The woman nodded.

"It's beautiful," Jordan said.

"It was," the woman admitted. "The walls are hand-polished elm. The fireplace works. Mr. Marland let me pick out the furniture that used to be here."

"It must have been great living in this room," Jordan suggested.

"It was," the woman replied. "But it was a long time ago and I didn't enjoy it long."

The old woman looked around the room and moved a decorative candle holder that sat on the fireplace mantel and said, "We must go. The security man will be back soon."

"Why did you do that?" Jordan asked. "Why do you keep moving things around?"

"You are nosy," the old woman replied. "But, you're observant. It's a little game I play. I come through every once and a while to check on the old place. When I do, I move things around to play with the security guards. This old house gets pretty eerie in the dark of the night when they're all alone. They think the place is haunted and my little mischief helps them think that. I know it's naughty, but I like doing it just the same."

Jordan smiled at the twinkle in the old woman's eye and the satisfaction she seemed to get at her little game.

"You have a beautiful smile, dear," the old woman observed.

Jordan immediately envisioned how goofy her large teeth must look and mumbled, "I don't think so."

The old woman studied Jordan for a moment and said, "You don't think much of yourself, do you?"

Jordan winced at the woman's blunt observation and muttered, "No ma'am, I guess not."

"Why not?" the woman asked.

"My teeth are too big, my elbows are bony, and my legs are longer than the rest of my body put together."

The old woman laughed softly and said, "It's hard being young...I remember. You're a pretty young girl and all your parts will fit into place one of these days—sooner than you think. You'll be prettier than that girl in the painting downstairs."

"I don't know about that?" Jordan smiled.

"I do," the old woman quickly replied. "That's the only advantage to being so old. You have a good sense about how things will turn out. Now follow me, and we'll get out of here before being found out."

Jordan followed the woman as she went into the long hallway connecting all the upstairs bedrooms. She led Jordan to an elevator with a polished oak door and leather walls. The elevator took them back to the lowest level and to the small room leading to the tunnel. The old woman moved a few more items around before pulling out her small flashlight and heading down the dark, curving tunnel.

"What's that?" Jordan said, as she noticed ghostly, strange-looking footprints in the damp cement.

The old woman laughed softly, as the sound reverberated down the long tunnel.

"It's me," the woman giggled. "I hadn't noticed that in years—no wonder the security guard doesn't like to come down the tunnel."

Jordan rubbed the wet cement to see that the footprints were lightly etched in the concrete.

"When Mr. Marland built this tunnel, I was anxious to be the first through," the woman explained. "I borrowed a pair of Mr. Marland's boots and walked the entire length. I didn't notice until days later that I had stepped on the concrete before it had completely cured leaving these footprints. I'm not sure

Mr. Marland ever noticed, which is strange, since he was such a stickler about every aspect of this house. Imagine those footprints being here after all those years."

The two walked the length of the tunnel and Jordan felt the fresh outside air as she exited the dank tunnel. The old woman shut the door behind her.

"Run along and I'll talk to you later," the old woman instructed.

Jordan obeyed and headed up the slight hill to the walkway above the boathouse. It was getting dark and she knew she needed to get home, but she did not want to be rude to the old woman. Walking back down the hill, Jordan looked into the boathouse and could not see Lydie.

"Miss Marland," she called out softly.

The calls echoed against the stone walls of the boathouse, but the old woman was nowhere in sight. Jordan ran up the hill to get a better vantage point and then back to the entrance to the tunnel. The door to the tunnel was locked, but there was no sign of the old woman. Jordan searched for a few more minutes, before heading home in the darkening evening. As she walked to the front gate, she looked back at the huge mansion and tried to determine where she had been on her trip inside. The property looked vacant, and she could see no sign of the strange old woman with whom she had spent her afternoon. With a shrug of her shoulder, Jordan headed home.

CHAPTER 11

Darkness threatened to overtake dusk by the time Jordan turned the corner to walk down 13th Street and toward her house. Halfway down the street, Jordon noticed a large pickup truck parked in front of her house. Her heart raced as she recognized the truck belonging to Chloe Beck's father. Chloe had been Jordan's best friend in Stillwater. Jordan ran as fast as she dared in the dim light, eager to see her friend.

To Jordan's horror, the truck began to pull away from the house. She waved frantically, but the truck accelerated steadily as it passed her.

"Wait!" Jordan screamed, but her cries were not heard.

As the truck drove away slowly, Jordan looked carefully for Chloe, but there was no one in the passenger seat. Jordan was out of breath from her short run, and a smile subconsciously came across her face as she realized Chloe must be at her house.

As Jordan approached the house however, she could tell something was not right. There was no sign of Chloe and Jordan caught a glimpse of her mother sulking into the house.

"Where is she?" Jordan asked quickly, still breathing hard from her short sprint.

"Who?" Barbara Bennett replied.

"Chloe," Jordan said impatiently. "I saw her dad's truck."

Barbara looked past Jordan and down the now vacant street before saying, "Chloe's not here."

A disappointed Jordan asked, "Why didn't she come with her dad?"

"I don't know," Barbara answered. "He was just in town and stopped by."

"I'm supposed to go see her," Jordan added. "You should have stopped him so I could have gone to see her."

Barbara sighed heavily and said, "It's not that simple. I couldn't just ask him to take you back to Stillwater."

"Of course you could," Jordan bluntly stated. "You said I could go see Chloe. I've been good."

"I know, dear," Barbara Bennett admitted. "But I can't take you right now."

"That's why I could have gone with Mr. Beck," Jordan insisted.

"That would have been rude," Barbara replied.

"No!" Jordan shouted back. "It would have been an inconvenience to you!"

"I'm doing the best I can," her mother sighed.

"That's not good enough!" Jordan huffed.

"Listen!" an angry Barbara Bennett replied. "I'm trying to keep this family together, earn a living, and go to school...without a lot of help from you. I'm doing all I can and taking you to Chloe is something I can't handle right now!"

Barbara regretted her hasty response, but was in no mood to deal with her daughter's attitude.

"You can't handle me being happy!" Jordan shot back.

Barbara tried to ignore the insult and said as calmly as she could, "Why don't you make friends with Linda Pelletier. She seems nice and you two have some things in common."

"What?" Jordan whined. "We're both social outcasts. You can't stand that Chloe and I are best friends and you don't have anyone. You're ruining my life. I hate you!"

Jordan stormed through the house and slammed the door to her room. She expected her angry mother to follow. Jordan prepared for the scolding, or grounding, or beating that was sure to come. As Jordan cowered in her room, the quietness was unnerving. Her mother did not come to her room. Jordan's relief was soon replaced by guilt as she listened to her mother sobbing outside her door. Jordan wanted to say she was sorry, but she could not. Her two week truce with her mother was over and Jordan knew there would be consequences for her harsh words.

Jordan had unsettling dreams about the quarrel with her mother. She was angry, confused, and frightened at her mother's response. All she wanted to do was see her friend Chloe.

Why couldn't her mother see how unhappy she was? Jordan thought. Why couldn't her mother see how much she needed a friend—needed Chloe?

That night, Jordan tossed and turned in an uneasy sleep until she woke up at the end of one of her strange dreams. Jordan looked at the clock reading 4:30 AM and knew what she had to do. Jordan flipped her pillow to the cool side and finally fell into a deep, peaceful sleep knowing her plan would help her get what she wanted. Jordan also believed her scheme might keep her mother happy—at least for a while.

CHAPTER 12

Jordan tried to be on her best behavior the next day and even helped with chores around the house. She was surprised she was not punished for her outburst the previous evening, but her mother seemed distant and distracted. Jordan did not mind, as long as she could keep on her mother's good side for a few more days.

The October days started with cool mornings followed by warm pleasant afternoons. Halloween was a couple of weeks away, but Brett's friends were already telling ghost stories and making plans for one of their favorite nights. Jordan made regular trips to the Marland Mansion the next few days and hoped to see Lydie again. The odd, old woman held a strange fascination for Jordan. She wanted to learn more about the secrets of the mansion and hear more stories about the woman's charmed life of big parties, fox hunts, and horseback riding. Jordan had not seen the old woman for several days, however, and entertained herself by watching the boys play sports and studying the exterior idiosyncrasies of the mansion.

"What'cha doin'?" a whiny voice asked, which interrupted her daydreaming.

Jordan jumped at the disruption. She had not noticed Jody Winkle had snuck up behind her. Although teachers at school called him Jody, most kids simply knew him as Winkie Dink— a nickname that seemed to fit. Winkie Dink was an obnoxious oddball that rode a ten-speed bicycle over the eastside of town. He was overweight, overbearing, and overblown. Although he was in the same grade as her brother Brett, Winkie Dink preferred to pester the younger kids in the neighborhood. Winkie Dink had never done anything to Jordan, but she was not excited to have his company.

"Nothing," Jordan assured.

"Like my bike?" Winkie asked.

"It's okay," Jordan apathetically replied. "You've shown it to me before."

"Oh yeah," he nodded. "I got it last Christmas. A kid stole it once, but the cops got it back."

"Humm," Jordan groaned, as she tried to make out some carvings on the mansion's wall.

"You're B.B.'s little sister, right?" Winkie asked.

"Yeah," Jordan answered.

"Cool," Winkie replied. "Is he going to try for varsity football next year?"

"I guess," Jordan shrugged.

"He better," Winkie suggested in an authoritative tone that was nearly humorous combined with his high pitched, nasal voice. "He's the only thing the freshmen got this year."

"Brett will do what he wants," Jordan assured him.

Winkie Dink looked over his shoulder and said, "I gotta go. See you later JorDAN."

Jordan rolled her eyes when he pronounced her name like J.J. Reynolds. J.J. could say "JorDAN" in a way that was teasing and fun. Winkie Dink was just annoying.

The fat boy grunted as he struggled to get his bicycle moving and Jordan was relieved. In a moment, Jordan saw Brad Cooper walking toward her.

"You here by yourself?" Brad asked.

"Winkie Dink was here, but he finally left," Jordan answered.

"Oh," Brad replied. "What are you doing?"

"Looking at the house," Jordan replied. "I think I like this view of the north terrace the best."

"Why?" Brad smiled, as he too began looking at the details of the house.

"I don't know," Jordan confessed. "I like all the carvings and the odd angles."

Jordan had been looking at some wafer-like stone structures surrounding a staircase to an upstairs patio. A circular overlook adorned the corner at the top of the stairs with some letters Jordan did not understand.

"What does that mean?" Jordan asked, as she pointed at the circular overlook with letters carved in the stone, "DOMUS SVA EST VNICVIQUE TVISSIMVM REFVGIVM."

"I have no idea," Brad confessed.

"Have you seen that old woman around?" Jordan asked.

"What old woman?" Brad replied.

"The old woman that hangs out around here," Jordan explained. "She wears weird clothes—lime colored raincoat, purple pants, and usually tennis shoes."

"No," Brad confessed. "I know who you're talking about, but I've not seen her around."

"She would know," Jordan stated.

"Know what?" J.J. Reynolds interrupted. "That Coop's up here trying to pick up B.B.'s sister?"

"Shut up!" Brad Cooper angrily replied.

"Ewww!" J.J. Reynolds teased. "It must be true!"

"What's true?" Brett asked, as he walked up.

"This is going to be hard to take, B.B.," J.J. Reynolds smiled.

"Shut up!" Brad Cooper demanded.

As Brad Cooper grappled with J.J. Reynolds, the taller J.J. held him at arm's length and said, "Coop's over here romancing your sister."

"Cut it out, J.J.," Brett Bennett groaned. "Coop's just bein' nice."

"Real nice," J.J. said in an exaggerated tone.

"Don't listen to him, Coop," Brett suggested. "He's just trying to rile you up."

Brad Cooper quit shoving J.J. Reynolds and stepped back without saying another word.

J.J. Reynolds, seeing he had pushed a little too far, changed the subject and asked, "So, what are you doing, JorDAN?"

Jordan smiled slightly at J.J.'s pet name for her and said, "I'm studying the house."

"What for?" J.J. smirked. "Is there a test or something?"

"No," Jordan giggled. "I was inside the other day and was trying to figure out how the outside matched up with the inside."

"When have you been inside?" her brother Brett asked in a concerned tone.

Jordan did not answer for a second before admitting, "The woman that hangs around here took me in."

"What woman?" Brett questioned.

"You've seen her," Jordan replied. "She's around here sometimes when you're playing—she wears weird clothes?"

"I've seen her," Brad Cooper interjected.

"Forget about the old woman," J.J. Reynolds interrupted. "How did you get in?"

"She took me through a tunnel," Jordan answered. "A secret tunnel."

The boys studied her a moment, trying to determine if she was serious.

With his sly smirk, J.J. asked, "Secret tunnel?"

Jordan looked around nervously before saying, "In the boathouse—the one with the walkway over it. Inside there's a tunnel. She took me through the tunnel."

The boys looked at each other before sprinting down the slight hill to the building. J.J. led the way while the others followed. The boys examined the three arches, looking for anything looking like a secret passage.

"How did you know this was a boathouse?" Brett asked. "I wouldn't have known a lake was here."

"The woman said there used to be several lakes around the house," Jordan explained. "She also said there was an island. This is where the canoes were stored."

"There's no secret passage," J.J. stated.

"It's there," Jordan insisted, pointing at the locked door.

J.J. walked to the heavy plank door and tugged on the padlock.

"This is not secret," J.J. fumed. "It's just a door."

"Where do you think this door would go to?" Brad Cooper asked. "This whole thing is below ground level that direction."

J.J. studied the location of the door again, before nodding in agreement.

"You say it goes to the house?" Brad asked.

"Yeah," Jordan replied. "The tunnel's long and wide. There's a creepy echo and everything."

Shaking the locked door, J.J. asked, "How did you break in?"

"We didn't," Jordan explained. "The woman had a key and a flashlight. She took me in, showed me around, and then we left."

Jordan walked toward the second arch and continued, "She was standing here when I walked up the hill. I turned back around and she was gone."

"Like a ghost?" J.J. asked.

"She's not a ghost," Jordan insisted. "I've seen her several times. Ask Brad."

"Hold on a minute," Brett interrupted. "Forget about ghosts, there's no such thing."

"Is too," J.J. insisted. "I've talked to the security guy and he's told me all about the strange things happening at this place."

Jordan giggled, thinking of the old woman's trick of moving random items, and caught the attention of the boys.

"I don't want to hear about any ghost or goblins," Brett insisted. "I want to know about this woman."

All the boys focused on Jordan, which made her feel nervous and important at the same time.

"Her name's Lydie," Jordan began. "I saw her a couple of weeks ago. She seemed odd, but nice enough. Mr. Grumman was here one day following her and he told me her name."

"You talked to Mr. Grumpy?" J.J. asked.

Jordan nodded.

"He glares at me every time I walk by his place," J.J. fumed.

"Forget about Mr. Grumman," Brett interrupted. "Who's this Lydie?"

"Mr. Grumman said the old woman used to live in the house—many years ago when it was first built," Jordan explained. "She came to live with her rich aunt and uncle. They adopted her and her brother. The house is amazing! It's beautiful and there's all kinds of secret passages and things. The old woman knows every inch of the house. She goes in and moves things around to mess with the caretaker and the security guy. That's why I was laughing."

"There's your ghost," Brett said to J.J. Reynolds.

"Aww," J.J. protested. "I don't believe a word of it, JorDAN. I haven't noticed any old woman and I don't see any secret tunnel. I think you've made up the whole story! Why would a woman that lived in a house like this have to sneak in? Even if there is a woman, which I doubt, there's no way you could know that she used to live here."

"Can too!" Jordan rebutted.

"How?" J.J. challenged.

"When I was in the house," Jordan explained, "she took me to this huge ballroom. In the room was a painting of a young woman and it was her! She's all old and everything now, but it was her. I can tell."

"Jordan," Brett interjected. "You know Mom doesn't like you talking to strangers."

"Mom doesn't like a lot of things," Jordan retorted. "Besides—the old woman's my friend. She knows stuff."

"What kind of stuff?" a cynical J.J. asked.

"Girl stuff," Jordan replied.

The boys laughed and J.J. said in a mocking tone, "Oh, it must be wonderful to talk about tea and shopping and fairytales."

"Knock it off, J.J.," Brett insisted. "Seriously, Jordan. What do you know about this woman?"

Jordan bit her bottom lip nervously and answered, "Not much—just what I've learned from her. I know she moved here when she was my age. They had big parties. When she grew up, handsome young men came from everywhere just to see her."

Out of the corner of her eye, Jordan could see J.J. making mocking gestures.

Jordan ignored him and continued, "They had fox hunts and horses—her father built this castle for a home."

"Why doesn't she live here, then?" Brett asked.

Jordan's forehead wrinkled as she considered the question.

"I don't know," she finally replied.

"Something happened," Jordan continued, speaking almost to herself. "I don't know what, though. It must have been bad. She hasn't said. She has just talked about the parties and the fun stuff."

Jordan thought a moment longer, before saying, "Mr. Grumman said something happened. I don't remember what he said, though. There was a statue...a statue of a woman. It got lost or broken, I can't remember which, but he was asking me if the woman knew where it was."

"Did she?" J.J. asked excitedly.

"No," Jordan replied. "She doesn't like questions. She just tells me things."

"That statue's got to be valuable," J.J. said eagerly. "And it's got to be around here somewhere or else Mr. Grumpy wouldn't be looking for it."

None of the boys could argue with J.J.'s logic.

Looking at Jordan, J.J. said, "You've got to find out where it's at. I bet there's other things hidden as well. There had to be art and jewelry. Something happened. If she had to hide the statue, you know she had to hide other stuff. They could be buried right here! Right where she said there used to be a lake!"

"I don't know," Jordan skeptically replied.

"You don't know, yet," J.J. smiled, "but you'll find out."

CHAPTER 13

"I know what it means!" an excited Brad Cooper smiled.

Jordan did not realize Brett's friend was talking to her at first. Several boys had come by the house to play basketball in the driveway.

"Huh?" Jordan finally muttered after noticing that none of the other boys could have possibly heard Brad.

"The words 'DOMUS SVA EST VNICVIQUE TVISSIMVM REFVGIVM' carved into the mansion," Brad explained.

"Oh," Jordan replied.

She had almost forgotten the carved letters she had seen.

"What does it mean?" Jordan asked.

"I figured out the words in a Latin dictionary," Brad replied. "Mrs. Flowers, the Latin teacher, helped with the grammar and said it meant, 'A man's house is his castle.'"

Jordan smiled and said, "That makes sense because the house literally is a castle."

"What are you two talking about?" J.J. Reynolds interrupted.

J.J. and Brett had been playing a game of one-on-one basketball in the driveway while Brad Cooper talked to Jordan about the translation. J.J. had stripped off his pullover sweatshirt and stood in his plain white tee shirt, even though the autumn breeze was cool. Brett, somewhat perturbed at the interruption to the game, came to investigate as well.

"Nothing," Brad Cooper claimed.

"You're always talking about nothing to B.B.'s sister," J.J. teased.

Before Brad could respond, Jordan said, "Brad translated the saying on the mansion."

"What saying?" a suddenly interested J.J. Reynolds asked.

"There's a carving on the mansion," Jordan explained.

"A carving?" J.J. sneered. "There's carvings all over that place."

"These were letters," Brad interjected. "It says in Latin, 'A man's house is his castle.'"

"What do you think it means?" J.J. quizzed.

"A lot of people say, 'Their house is their castle,' but the guy that built that house tried to build a real castle," Brad explained.

"Is that all?" J.J. asked.

"I guess," Brad replied.

"Maybe it's some kind of clue," J.J. offered.

"A clue to what?" Brett asked.

"To the treasure," J.J. answered.

"What treasure?" Brett scoffed.

"JorDAN talked about a missing statue the other day," J.J. explained. "A place like that, there's got to be all kinds of treasure hidden around. I figured maybe there were some clues."

"The place was built like a castle," Brad added. "My mom said it used to have lakes around the whole house like a moat. It sure looks like a castle."

"You guys have too much imagination," the practical Brett replied. "Granted, I'm not from around here, but even I know the old place was a school for as long as most people could remember. I don't think you'll find much treasure there."

"I know someone who would know," Jordan claimed.

The boys stopped their banter to look at Jordan.

"Who?" Brett asked, impatiently.

"That ghost lady JorDAN's always talking about," J.J. sneered.

"She's not a ghost," Jordan reacted. "Her name's Lydie Marland and she used to live in that house."

J.J. mocked, "So, you're just going to go up to this old lady and ask, 'Hey, Lydie, where's all your stuff hidden?'"

Jordan had not thought about how impractical her suggestion had been. She only had a few conversations with

Lydie and the woman always seemed resistant to answering any questions.

"There's someone else who would know," Brad Cooper claimed.

"Who?" J.J. asked.

"Mr. Grumpy would know," Brad said.

Brett and J.J. snickered at the idea.

"Really," Brad defended himself. "My mom says he's a real expert on history and stuff from around here. He used to work on restoring the old place. He would know."

"I'd rather ask the ghost lady," J.J. huffed. "That old man hates me."

"Maybe it's because you're always pestering him," Brett suggested.

Before the boys could continue their discussion, a shiny, new pickup truck interrupted them as it crept slowly down the street, as if searching for something.

"I got to go," J.J. hastily said, as he started walking north.

"Where are you going?" Brett asked.

J.J. did not answer, but walked away and slipped between the house and into the Bennett's backyard where an alley ran behind the house.

The truck moved slowly up the street before stopping in front of the Bennett house. A tall man stepped out of the pickup and looked over the neighborhood behind his dark sunglasses.

"Who's that?" Brad asked.

"I have no idea," Brett confessed.

The man walked to the house, ignoring Brett, Brad, and Jordan. He looked into the window before walking to the front door and knocking forcefully.

"Can I help you?" Brett finally asked.

The man looked over his sunglasses and showed dark, penetrating eyes.

"Is your mom or dad around?" the stranger finally asked.

"No," Brett answered.

The man appeared disappointed and looked around the property once more. The man reached into his pocket and produced an envelope and a business card.

"Give this to them," the man instructed. "They're a month behind on the rent. Have your folks call me tonight. Tell them I'll be back with an eviction notice by the end of the week if I don't have the rent."

A humiliated Brett meekly said, "Yes, sir."

The man studied the house once more as if trying to see if an adult would come out before walking to his truck and driving away.

"I better go," Brad said awkwardly.

"Yeah," Brett sighed. "See you Coop."

Brad Cooper nodded and walked away from the Bennett house to his home in the more prosperous neighborhood close to the Marland Mansion.

"Let's get inside," Brett instructed, as he led his younger sister by the arm into the small house.

"What was that all about?" Jordan worriedly asked.

"Nothing," Brett assured.

Brett did not say more about the incident, but Jordan noticed his silence as he went to his room and listened to his records alone. Jordan did not press him further and let her brother have his space. She could tell the incident embarrassed him in front of his friends, but she did not know what to say to make him feel better. Jordan often felt self-conscious about her family situation, but had not shown much empathy for the challenges her mother faced. Jordan had noticed "Past-Due" stamped on many of the bills coming to the house, but that was an adult problem she did not understand. She knew her mother fussed often about money and about her children being wasteful, but Jordan never suspected her family had trouble paying bills.

As Jordan sat in the front room worrying about her brother, she quietly began resenting families like the Coopers and Pelletiers that had perfect lives in their perfect houses.

Why do I and my family have to deal with all these problems? Jordan thought to herself.

Brett did not come out for supper, so Jordan ate a peanut butter and jelly sandwich. She loved peanut butter and jelly, but for some reason the sandwich made her feel poor this evening. She finished the sandwich, but did not feel satisfied. The hunger was not with her appetite, however, but in her soul. Jordan began doing something she had become too familiar with the past months—she felt sorry for herself.

When Barbara Bennett showed up late in the night from her job, Jordan did not have confidence that her mother could make her feel better.

"Hey, Jordan," Barbara Bennett smiled, putting her purse and keys on a small table by the door.

"Hey," Jordan muttered.

"What's wrong?" Barbara asked as she stepped to her daughter and touched her forehead.

Barbara was used to her daughter being defiant, being angry, and even being unreasonable, but she was not prepared to see her daughter look hopeless.

"Nothing," Jordan replied.

Brett came out of his bedroom when he heard his mother enter the house.

"Hey, honey," Barbara smiled as she continued to rub her daughter's forehead.

Brett stepped stoically toward his mother and said, "A man told me to give this to you."

Brett handed the notice to his mother and watched her carefully. Any semblance of good cheer Barbara Bennett had immediately vanished. Her cheeks turned pale as she read the summons while her children watched anxiously.

"Is everything okay?" Brett asked, although he knew the answer.

"It's fine," Barbara lied. "I must have forgotten to mail the rent check his month. I'll get paid Friday and things will be fine."

Barbara put on a fake smile to comfort her children, but they were old enough to know things were far from fine. Her children also sensed their mother did not need further questions about the family's finances. Jordan hugged her mother, which she had believed she was too old to do, and headed to bed. Brett watched his mother; wanting to help but not knowing how. In a few minutes he retreated back to his room. Barbara Bennett sat silently in her front room for a long time. She thought she could pay the rent, but had less faith that she could solve all her family's problems.

CHAPTER 14

Jordan's empathy for her mother was short lived. Barbara Bennett managed to pay the rent, but when Jordan asked for a new coat to replace the embarrassing one she wore each day, Barbara gave her a lecture about the family's economic realities. Barbara made the mistake of muttering that their financial woes would be over if Jordan's father would send some money. Jordan defended her father, which only caused her mother to make that pitiful scowling face that irritated her daughter further. The conversation ended with Jordan slamming the door as she marched defiantly to the bus.

By the time Jordan reached school, she was calmed by an idea that had been brewing in her head the past weeks. Jordan had been working on a plan to see her friend Chloe and hoped the pieces would fall into place today. Chloe would know what to say to make Jordan feel better. Chloe would understand. Linda Pelletier had tried to be a friend, but Jordan knew the girl with the perfect family could never be a true friend like Chloe.

Jordan sat alone in the cafeteria, nervously waiting for Linda Pelletier. The typical angst of sitting alone in the junior high cafeteria was overshadowed by her anxiety about Linda's late appearance. Several kids looked like they might take the seat next to Jordan, but none did. Jordan finally saw Linda enter the cafeteria next to the last in line.

"Where have you been?" Jordan asked, as Linda took the seat next to her.

"By the time I got out of algebra, the line was already backed up," Linda explained. "I was almost done with my homework, so I decided to finish before getting in line."

"Cool," Jordan replied as she picked at the last of her peas left on the plate.

"What'cha been up to?" Linda asked.

"You know, the same old same old," Jordan chatted.

"Nothing changes in this place," Linda affirmed. "You get your algebra done in class?"

"Not quite," Jordan confessed, "but it shouldn't take long when I get home."

There was an awkward silence in the girls' conversation when Jordan asked, "Are you going to the game this weekend?"

Linda looked somewhat surprised at the question and said, "Yeah—didn't think you followed football unless J.J. Reynolds was playing."

Jordan laughed uneasily and replied, "Oh—I've been trying to broaden my horizons. I hear State's playing Kansas this weekend."

Jordan had little interest in football, although her father sometimes watched the games. She did, however, have an interest in the teams playing in Stillwater. Jordan had read in the paper that Oklahoma State was playing Kansas and knew Linda's parents often went to the games.

"Yeah," Linda smiled. "It ought to be a better game than last week."

Jordan did not know or care about last week's game. She knew Linda had once invited her to a game and hoped she could get another invitation without having to ask directly.

Jordan struggled to think of something to say and asked, "I guess Kansas has a pretty good team this year?"

"I don't think Kansas ever has a good team," Linda grinned. "That's why we may win."

Jordan smiled at Linda's enthusiasm and waited nervously for an invitation to go to a game.

"We need a win after the last two weeks," Linda continued.

Jordan nodded and looked as interested as she could, although she had no idea what had happened the previous two weeks.

"Hey," Linda said, as if she had an epiphany. "Why don't you come to a game sometime?"

"That'd be fun," Jordan replied, trying not to appear too anxious.

"We usually have tickets," Linda smiled. "I'll have to check, but I'll know tomorrow."

"That'd be great," Jordan nodded. "I'd love to see a game."

Jordan hoped she would get an invite to the Kansas game, but did not really care which game.

Jordan went home that evening to tell her mother that she might have a chance to go to a football game. Barbara Bennett was excited that Jordan got an invitation and was making a new friend, especially one from church.

The next day, an excited Linda informed Jordan that her family did have extra tickets and would leave early to eat out before the game.

The Pelletier family arrived at Jordan's house a little after nine o'clock. Jordan was out the door before their car came to a complete stop. Mrs. Pelletier got out of the car to talk to Jordan's mother, but Barbara Bennett was already at work. Jordan hurried into the backseat of the Pelletier family's Jeep Grand Cherokee. The vehicle still had a new car smell.

Mrs. Pelletier had a seemingly endless list of questions she asked, while Mr. Pelletier clicked through radio stations trying to find any information about the game, which kicked-off early in the afternoon. Jordan patiently answered all of Mrs. Pelletier's questions, trying to keep a straight face as Linda would roll her eyes at her mother's prying. Mrs. Pelletier was very polite, but Jordan felt uneasy at questions that sometimes seemed to be thinly veiled inquiries about the Bennett family dynamics.

Mr. Pelletier appeared uninterested in listening to the women talk. He would, however, interject some of his unique insights and strong opinions about Big Eight football when his wife became too interested in their young guest. Jordan could tell Mr. Pelletier did not like the Oklahoma or Nebraska football teams that had beaten Oklahoma State the previous two weeks. Jordan apathetically listened. Her brother Brett had become a big Oklahoma fan since moving to Ponca City, but Jordan did not really understand all of the fuss. The conversation and questions, however, made the trip go quickly and in less than an hour, Stillwater was in sight.

The Pelletier family attended many of the games. They found a place to park a couple of blocks from the stadium and met their son Steve, who was a freshman, for lunch. Jordan was glad to have Steve eat with the family. Mrs. Pelletier quizzed him about campus life, which made Jordan feel as if the woman had less time to question her. Linda made Jordan almost laugh a couple of times by mimicking her mother when her parents were not watching. After lunch, Steve left to meet some friends and the Pelletiers headed to the stadium.

Jordan had never been to a college football game in person and had only watched a few minutes when her father or brother happened to have a game on the television. The stadium looked like a rusted erector set with huge metal beams painted orange holding up the seats above. Although Jordan did not watch football much, she could understand the game-day attraction, with band music playing, the smell of hotdogs, and the overall festive atmosphere. The Pelletier family had seats close to the thirty yard-line, but there were plenty of places to sit in the large stadium. Most people were clad in orange or black, with a few wearing blue in the corner of the stadium. Jordan was sure she was the only person wearing yellow. After Mr. Pelletier's rant about the Sooners and Cornhuskers, Jordan was thankful she had not chosen to wear red.

Jordan patiently watched the game while studying the Pelletier family. After a few minutes, Jordan excused herself to get a soda. Linda offered to go with her and Mrs. Pelletier almost insisted, but Jordan managed to convince them to let her go alone. Jordan's plan had been to slip out of the stadium and walk quickly to Chloe's house less than a mile away. She figured that if she hurried, she could get back to the game and tell Mrs. Pelletier that she had gotten turned around in the stadium and walked to the wrong side.

The streets were nearly empty as she exited the stadium and walked swiftly to the east. Jordan had one major street to cross and then a short walk through a subdivision of nice brick homes to get to Chloe's house. Jordan was sure she could easily make it there and back.

As Jordan walked quickly, her excitement at her adventure was tempered by her anger at her mother. If her mother had taken a half-day to drive her or if she had allowed Chloe to come visit, Jordan would not have had to take advantage of Linda's hospitality to get a ride to Stillwater. A smile appeared on Jordan's face as she thought of the good times she had shared with Chloe in the past. They had practically grown up together and were more like sisters than friends. Their parents had been best friends and Jordan had spent many hours at Chloe's house.

Jordan's heart sank as the house came into view. She did not see a car out front and worried that maybe the family had gone somewhere for the weekend. Usually, Mr. Beck's pickup truck was parked in the driveway. The Becks had a garage, however, and Jordan prayed that someone was home.

Jordan knocked on the door and waited anxiously. She breathed a sigh of relief when she thought she heard voices from inside. In a few seconds, the door opened and Jordan stood face to face with her friend, Chloe.

"Jordan?" Chloe greeted her. "What are you doing here?"

"Chloe!" Jordan squealed. "I'm in town for the game and decided to stop by!"

"It's great to see you," Chloe replied.

Chloe looked nervously into the house before stepping outside.

"How are you doing?" Chloe asked. "I was afraid you'd be mad."

"It's just my mother," Jordan replied. "She drives me crazy sometimes, but we're managing."

A confused Chloe looked at Jordan but did not speak. Jordan smiled, happy just to be on the front porch with her friend. The next sound Jordan heard, however, changed her mood—forever.

"Who's there?" the familiar male voice shouted from inside the house.

Jordan watched the terrified Chloe become speechless. Chloe looked down at her shoes in awkward silence.

In another moment, Jordan's father called out again, "Who's at the door?"

Before Jordan could speak, her father stood at the door.

"Jordan?" her father muttered.

Jordan wanted to run and hug him. She wanted to take him into her arms and bring him back into her life, but she was old enough to know that would never happen now.

"I thought you were my friend," Jordan whispered harshly to Chloe.

"I am," a tearful Chloe replied.

"How long has he been here?" Jordan asked.

"Now, Jordan—" her father began.

Jordan was numb. She could not feel anything, and she kept her eyes on Chloe while trying to forget her father existed.

"About a month," Chloe whispered.

"Jordan," her father tried to console her.

Jordan would have liked to have had something to say to her father. She would have liked to have hurt him as badly as he had hurt her.

"I've got to go," Jordan finally muttered.

"Jordan, wait," her father pleaded.

"I've got to get back to the game," Jordan replied, as she walked away from the house.

Her father stepped onto the front porch, but did not have his shoes. Jordan kept walking as her father continued to plead for her to stop. When he went into the house, Jordan ran. Tears filled her eyes and she felt as if the earth were spinning beneath her. Jordan looked back a couple of times to see if her father would come after her. She wanted him to come, but she wanted to get away. She sprinted across the busy street and began to cry uncontrollably. Jordan looked one more time to see if her father was coming. She could not see him and turned down a residential street a couple of blocks from the stadium. Jordan could hear the crowd in the nearby stadium, but she felt incredibly alone. She slowed to a staggered walk as emotions overwhelmed her.

Jordan did not know what to do or where to go for a few minutes. She did not think she could go back to the Pelletiers with tears in her eyes. Jordan could not face anybody. She continued to walk down the lonely streets, hoping someone would come for her, but sure she would be on her own, forever. Jordan had thought of running away for many weeks, but always held some hope that her family would get back together or that at least she could stay with her father for a while. Now her father had moved in with Chloe's mother and Jordan's world seemed out of control. Jordan did not know what to do but walk, so she wandered alone with the roar of the nearby crowd in the football stadium fading with each step.

CHAPTER 15

Jordan walked aimlessly through the side streets surrounding the university. She looked over her shoulder with conflicted feelings and emotions. She wanted to avoid her father, but desperately wanted him to come for her. A couple of vehicles passed, but none she recognized. Jordan's heart raced and then fell when it became evident her father was not coming. The fact she did not know what kind of car her father drove was a painful reminder of how separated she had become from his life.

Jordan lost track of time as she wandered the neighborhood. She felt hurt, betrayed, and abandoned. When Jordan realized she needed to get back to the game, she lethargically stepped toward the stadium. She was not anxious to be reunited with the Pelletiers. They reminded her of a family life that now seemed lost. As Jordan started back, she became anxious. She walked faster as anxiety turned to panic.

Crowds now flooded the streets surrounding the stadium. Jordan realized the game was over. The jubilant crowd indicated the home team had won. Jordan fought against the crowd, eager to find the Pelletiers. Wiping her teary eyes, she tried to concoct a story to explain her long absence. Jordan searched for a familiar face, but she seemed invisible to the throng surrounding her. The disoriented girl tried to remember where the Pelletiers had parked, but she felt lost.

Jordan walked around the stadium trying to get her bearings. She went to half a dozen parking lots, but could not find any that looked familiar and could not locate the car. The crowd soon dissipated and Jordan felt truly alone. She began to cry and walked south across the campus past Sixth Street about a mile away. Jordan walked past the city's hospital and through the parking lot of an office building for a state agency. She continued several more blocks south on a street called Walnut, before stopping in front of a white frame house in need of paint.

The house was smaller than she had remembered. It looked vacant and lonely—almost as lonely as she felt. Jordan walked to the front step and flopped down with her head on her knees. As afternoon transitioned to evening, a chilly, fine mist made her hair damp and camouflaged her tear-streaked cheeks. Jordan was tired, hungry, and alone. Jordan could not think of anything to do but sit on the porch of her old house remembering how happy her family had once been.

The distinctive clanking of her mother's car rattled through the dark street. Feelings of rage were replaced by terror as Jordan thought of how angry her mother would be. Jordan had no one but her mother now. She knew that, but she did not look forward to the coming rant.

The car screeched to a squeaking halt and Jordan buried her head deeper into her knees. She could not bear to face her mother and wanted desperately to be invisible. Jordan heard the door open and listened as her mother's steps approached. Jordan braced for the scolding she deserved, but heard nothing but the soft brush of her mother's raincoat as Barbara Bennett took a seat next to her daughter. The only sound was the sobbing coming from her mother and the touch of her mother's arm gently cradling her.

Jordan sat motionless for a moment before peeking up at her mother's reddened and teary eyes.

"Are you okay?" her mother finally asked.

Jordan nodded before saying, "I guess you're mad."

"Worried," her mother softly replied. "Mrs. Pelletier called a couple of hours ago and was frantic. I thought you would be here. I came as soon as I could."

"How long have you known?" Jordan asked.

Barbara did not answer for a moment before saying, "About your father and Chloe's mom? A couple of months, I guess."

After a long pause, Barbara continued, "I didn't know how to tell you. I didn't want to make things worse. I didn't want you to hate me more than you do now."

Jordan listened and thought before saying, "I thought Chloe was my friend."

"Chloe didn't have anything to do with this dear," Barbara explained. "It was your father and her mother...I guess they thought...I don't know what they thought. I'm just sorry for you...I'm sorry you had to find out this way."

"Your father," Barbara Bennett continued with a frustrated tone. "He's always done what he wanted and didn't care much about how it hurts others. I should have seen that before—"

"Before you had me and Brett?" Jordan interrupted.

"No!" Barbara protested. "You and Brett are my life—my one joy. I—I wished I'd known how to make things better. I'm trying, I promise."

Jordan's sniffling tears now exploded into uncontrollable crying as she buried her head in her mother's shoulder and said, "I know."

After a while, Barbara Bennett said, "How about we get a bite to eat? I bet you're starved."

Jordan nodded and Barbara Bennett helped her daughter to their old car. After a phone call to the Pelletiers, they shared a hamburger together and talked about some of the things that had happened the past year. Jordan expected her mother to lash out at her ditching the Pelletiers, but it was the first serious conversation Jordan could remember having with her mother. She learned that her father and mother had been having problems before leaving Stillwater. The move to Ponca City was a desperate attempt to somehow save the family. Stillwater had too many bad memories for Barbara now and she would finish nursing school in the spring. For the first time, Jordan understood that Ponca City would be her home for a long time. She had always dreamed that life would return to what she believed to be normal. Today had been a harsh lesson in the reality of her situation.

The old car was warm and the rhythmic clanking of the engine soon put Jordan to sleep on the trip back to Ponca City. Jordan did not wake up until they pulled into the driveway. Her mother helped her out of the car and guided her into the house. Jordan was too big for her mother to lift, but Barbara Bennett held her daughter tightly as she guided the tired girl into her bed. Jordan enjoyed the soft touch of her mother and soon fell into a deep, but restless sleep.

CHAPTER 16

Barbara Bennett let her daughter fake an illness and miss church the next day, but Monday she made Jordan get on the bus for school. Jordan entered school with a sickening feeling of dread. Linda Pelletier had tried to be her friend, but she was now the person Jordan feared seeing the most. The morning had been miserable, as Jordan looked carefully down every hallway before scurrying to class. Jordan shared the same algebra class with Linda. Jordan sat on the front row and kept her eyes on the desk the whole period. When the bell rang, she walked quickly to the cafeteria without putting up her books in order to be the first in the lunch line.

Jordan awkwardly maneuvered her books while taking a seat in the corner of the cafeteria where she could put her back to everyone. Her plan was to eat quickly and get to a secluded part of the library before Linda spotted her. Jordan hoped she could continue this routine for another seven months until school dismissed for the summer.

Jordan took her last swig of milk when she heard Linda Pelletier say, "You used me, didn't you?"

Linda's tone was neither angry nor animated. Instead her voice was serious and composed.

Jordan did not know how to respond, but she knew how she felt. She had lied to Linda to get somewhere she thought she wanted to be. Linda tried to be her friend and Jordan had embarrassed her and her family.

"I'm sorry," Jordan finally muttered softly.

Linda surprised Jordan by taking a seat next to her and asking, "Are you all right?"

Jordan did not expect the question and shrugged her shoulders.

"I thought you had run away," Linda shared.

"I thought about it," Jordan confessed.

"Why?" Linda asked, in a non-accusatory tone of voice.

If Jordan's mother had asked these same questions, Jordan would have been agitated and defensive. Linda's genuine concern comforted Jordan. Linda sat silently after the question as if coaxing and daring Jordan to answer.

"I don't know," Jordan finally lied.

Linda tilted her head to listen without responding.

Jordan finally confessed, "I went to see a friend. My family—my family's been through a lot this year. Dad left—I don't think I realized that until Saturday. When I went to see my friend, I learned he had moved in with her mom."

"Get out of here!" Linda tried to comfort her. "That's bad."

Jordan nodded at Linda's attempt to console her and said, "I always thought Dad had left my mom—I've blamed her for a lot of things lately. Now I know he left me and my brother as much as he left Mom."

Jordan tried to compose herself, knowing she could not cry in the school cafeteria.

"Bummer," Linda sighed.

Linda's one word response accurately described Jordan's feelings. Jordan smiled slightly at the plain-looking Linda's succinct assessment of the situation.

"I thought I could sneak out of the game and get back before you guys missed me," Jordan explained. "Things got complicated, then I got lost. Were your parents mad?"

"Mom freaked," Linda smiled, showing her gleaming braces. "She noticed you were gone for a long time and went looking. She even had them announce your name at the game!"

"Oh, no," Jordan whispered.

"Then she really lost it," Linda continued. "She made us go to the car and we drove around looking for you. Mom was convinced you had been kidnapped. I tried to tell her that we needed to leave the car parked so you could find it, but she never listens to me. She finally called your mom in a panic. Your mom was pretty cool. She said she knew where you would be. I guess she was right."

"She found me," Jordan sighed.

"How did it go?" Linda asked. "Was it bad?"

"Mom was actually great," Jordan admitted. "I thought she would kill me—literally—but she just listened. She took me for a hamburger. It's the first time I haven't been angry with her since I can remember."

"Your mom's pretty cool," Linda replied.

Jordan snickered insincerely and said, "How?"

"You don't see it," Linda explained, "but I admire her. She's going to school, taking care of things—taking care of you. That's pretty cool."

"You're right," Jordan conceded. "Mom has been trying to keep things together. She was pretty cool Saturday."

Jordan was finished with her lunch, but Linda continued to pick at her food when Jordan asked, "How about you? Are you mad at me?"

"No," Linda shrugged. "Just let me know what's going on next time and don't think you're the only one in the world with worries."

"Deal," Jordan smiled.

The rest of the school day went better. Talking to Linda had been a big relief. Linda was easy to talk to and Jordan decided she needed that in her life this year. Jordan did not know if she and Linda would ever be best friends, but Linda was proving to be someone on whom she could count. Jordan walked home to the empty house after school, but somehow it seemed a little less lonely than the day before.

CHAPTER 17

Barbara Bennett managed to pay the rent. She tried not to complain about her husband or the money in front of her children, but the family's expenses threatened to overwhelm her. The back rent took most of her paycheck, and she resented her husband's irresponsibility. She took a small payday loan to pay the electric bill and at least had a place to live for another month. Barbara felt crippled with anxiety, but she was determined to keep her worries from her children.

"Jordan," Barbara pleaded. "Could you please pick up the front room while I'm at work? Brett's at TG&Y tonight and I need you. I have a clinical tomorrow afternoon."

"Sure," Jordan nonchalantly said, as she read a magazine.

Barbara rubbed her inattentive daughter's head and left for another long evening of work. Jordan finished her article and then looked around the cluttered room. She had all evening, but felt energetic. She turned up the volume on the radio and began cleaning the messy room. Jordan was singing loudly to one of her favorite songs when she was interrupted by an urgent knock on the door.

Jordan froze for a moment and her first instinct was to ignore the knocking and pretend no one was at home, but the blaring music could have easily been heard on the front porch. Cautiously, Jordan moved to the window to see who was at the door. Jordan let out a muffled squeal when she saw her father standing on the dark porch.

"Daddy!" Jordan excitedly cried as she opened the door to hug her father.

"Hey, Pumpkin," he said while gently holding his excited daughter.

"I knew you'd come back," Jordan cried.

Randle Bennett smiled at his daughter and said, "Is your mother around?"

"She's at work," Jordan beamed.

Her father looked confused so Jordan explained, "She's working part-time at the Git-n-Go out on the highway."

"Oh," Randle said with a nod. "Where's Brett?"

"He's doing some odd jobs at the TG&Y tonight," Jordan explained. "They're doing inventory."

"You're here by yourself?" her father asked.

Jordan nodded.

After an awkward silence, Randle Bennett said, "I'm glad to have some time to—to see you by yourself. I wanted to explain—about the other day."

Jordan felt like a stormy wind hit her in the face as sounds seemed muffled in an unreal ringing. She looked at her father, but had a feeling of dread and could not find any words to say.

"I—I didn't want you to find out that way," her father continued. "Things have been—complicated for the past few months. I've been trying to find myself and get some things straight in my head."

"So you're coming home?" Jordan hopefully asked.

Her father stepped away for a moment and looked out the front window to the dark street.

"Pumpkin, things aren't always that easy," Randle Bennett tried to explain.

"But you are coming home?" Jordan pleaded.

Randle Bennett turned to face his daughter and said, "We never know what the future holds. I've got to do what's right— for me and your mom."

"How about me?" Jordan asked.

"Of course you and Brett are the most important," Randle explained.

Before he could say more, the back door creaked open signaling Brett had returned for the evening.

"Brett?" Randle Bennett greeted his son as he stepped into the room.

"What are you doing here?" Brett coldly asked.

"I came to see you guys," Randle Bennett answered. "I thought your mother would be here, but Jordan says she's working tonight."

"She works most nights," Brett replied.

"That's what Jordan said," Randle acknowledged.

"She goes to school every day, too," Brett added.

Randle Bennett nodded slightly and asked, "When do you think she'll be home?"

"She'll be home about ten," Jordan offered.

"Oh," Randle said, trying to hide his disappointment. "Well—that's good. That'll give me some time to catch up with you guys. How's school?"

"Fine," Brett said.

"It stinks," Jordan shared. "I want to go back to Stillwater. No one likes me here and I don't really like them, either."

Randle Bennett swallowed hard and said, "Pumpkin, you've got to be able to make new friends wherever you go. Right Brett?"

Brett did not answer, but Jordan said, "I would just as soon make new friends back in Stillwater."

"I'm sure you'll make some friends," her father assured her. "This is a great town."

Jordan looked at her father for a moment before asking, "Why were you at Chloe's?"

Although Jordan knew the answer, she held a genuine hope that her father had a good explanation.

Randle looked at his two children and finally replied, "I—I go visit the Becks sometimes. I get pretty lonely and it's good to see old friends."

"You're not there to see the Becks," Brett charged. "We're not stupid. We know you're living with Chloe's mother."

Randle Bennett struggled to control a flash of anger at his son's accusations. Jordan knew Brett spoke the truth, but she had hoped for a different reason from her father.

"You don't know everything that's gone on," Randle Bennett defended himself. "Sometimes adults grow apart and—"

Before Randle Bennett could finish his statement, Brett turned to walk away.

"Where are you going?" his father asked.

"I've got homework to do and it's getting late," Brett said.

"You don't want to spend time with your old dad?" Randle Bennett asked.

"I've spent time with you," Brett dryly replied. "You've done things that are good for you without thinking much about how I felt about it and now I have some things to do myself."

Before Randle Bennett could protest, Brett abruptly left his father and sister alone in the front room.

"I guess that gives us more time to catch up, Pumpkin," Randle smiled.

Jordan nodded politely and tried to carry on a conversation with her father. She loved him and wanted desperately to say the right things. She had been angry at Brett's rudeness, but she also found it difficult to find much to say to her father. He had not been a part of her life for many months. She wanted to ask him the real reasons he had left them. She wanted to know what she could have done differently, but the conversation was sterile and awkward. As much as she wanted to understand her father, she felt like she was talking to a stranger instead of the man she had idealized the past year. When her mother returned, Jordan was temporarily relieved to end the clumsy conversation. The tension between her father and mother was immediate and unmistakable, however, and Jordan now wished that her father had left before Barbara Bennett had come home.

"What are you doing here?" Barbara curtly asked.

"I came to the see the kids," Randle Bennett explained. "And to see you."

"You've seen us," Barbara observed.

"You're not going to make this easy, are you?" Randle sighed.

Looking past her husband, Barbara said to her daughter, "Jordan, get ready for bed."

Jordan did not argue and took the opportunity to leave and head to the safety of her room. Before she could shut her bedroom door, however, her brother Brett slipped into her room.

"Are you okay?" Brett asked, with a sincere look of concern.

Jordan nodded and whispered, "What's going on?"

"I don't know," Brett replied. "I think we're about to find out, though."

For the next hour, the two children listened to the conversation in the front room through the wall in Jordan's room. Their parents talked in animated whispers that were hard to understand. As the conversation progressed, however, the soft murmurs became louder, emotional outbursts. By the time Randle Bennett explained that he had brought divorce papers the argument could have been heard in the next house.

The two adults traded accusations, ridicule, and threats. The anger about betrayed feelings and dashed dreams quickly turned to money. The volume increased as both parties pleaded for understanding while jabbing at each other. Jordan and Brett listened in painful silence. Both knew this result was likely after the past year, but they also had held some thread of hope. After tonight, there would be no turning back, as the couple who had once promised "until death do us part" now seethed with malice.

"You don't have to like it!" Randle Bennett finally screamed. "That's the way it is and you need to get on with your life!"

"I have!" Barbara cried back. "Every single day I get on with the life you ruined!"

The front door slammed and shortly after, the sound of screeching tires indicated their father had left. Brett, followed by Jordan, slipped out of the bedroom to see about his mother.

Barbara Bennett sat in quiet defeat. Her puffy eyes showed she had cried during much of the heated conversation, but she tried desperately to wipe her face before her children could see.

"I guess you heard that?" she moaned.

"Most of it," Brett confessed.

"I'm sorry for that," Barbara apologized.

"You don't need to be," Brett said. "It'll be okay."

Barbara tried to smile, but her face twisted pathetically as she said, "I'm not so sure."

Brett walked close to his mother and she reached up and hugged his arm.

"Your father brought the divorce papers, tonight," Barbara explained, although Brett and Jordan could easily deduce that from the conversation they had overheard the past hour. "I guess it's not a surprise, but it seems so final now. I've sworn I won't talk bad about your father in front of you, but he's sure making that hard."

"We're here for you, Mom," Brett assured her.

"I know you are," Barbara replied. "The only thing your father ever did that matters to me are you two. You're all I have now. Your father has moved in with Carol Beck—there's no going back now. We're on our own—forever."

Jordan wanted to comfort her mother, but could not think of anything helpful to say. She moved next to her brother Brett and Barbara Bennett hugged both of her children tightly as she bravely fought back tears. In a few minutes, she ordered her children to bed. The house was silent in another fifteen minutes, but Jordan was not sure anyone in the house actually slept that long, heartbreaking night.

CHAPTER 18

Halloween had long been Jordan's favorite holiday. She liked the costumes and the fact that Halloween did not have the awkward family time required by other holidays. After the painful reality of her crumbling family life, Jordan believed that getting lost in the masquerade of outlandish costumes would be a helpful diversion.

Jordan felt she was too old to go trick-or-treating, but when her mother insisted Brett take her to the Friday night football game, Jordan's disappointment vanished. Brett was not happy about having his kid sister tag along, but he did not dare defy his mother. It was Halloween night at the stadium in Ponca City and the band put on a show dressed in costumes. Brett insisted Jordan sit two full rows behind his friends, and they ignored her except for occasional teasing. Jordan did not mind—she felt a part of the group even if she was two rows removed.

"What's going on?" the pleasant voice of Linda Pelletier greeted Jordan from behind.

Jordan turned around to see Linda awkwardly stepping over a family at the end of the row to take a seat nearby.

"Not much," Jordan replied. "Just watching the halftime show and taking verbal abuse from my brother's gang."

Linda looked at the group of boys sitting two rows in front of Jordan.

"Why are you sitting up here?" Linda asked.

"Brett made me," Jordan pouted. "Mom made him take me. She doesn't like me at home by myself. Brett said I could come, but had to stay out of his way."

"How's things with your mom?" Linda asked.

"Pretty good," Jordan claimed. "She didn't really freak out or anything about my—side trip."

"Cool," Linda nodded.

Jordan did not dare tell Linda about the divorce papers her father had delivered. Jordan believed someone coming from a perfect family like Linda's could not possibly understand the humiliation of a broken family.

"Things have been pretty good this week," Jordan lied. "Mom and I won't be hanging out real soon, but she's giving me some space."

"I better get back to my seat," Linda said. "I saw you down here and thought I'd say hi."

"Thanks," Jordan smiled.

"There's another game this weekend, but I don't think my mom's up to you coming yet," Linda smirked.

"I bet she'll never be ready for me to go again," Jordan replied.

"Ah, don't worry about it," Linda smiled. "Mom'll get over it. Maybe we can try a basketball game sometime."

"Thanks," Jordan nodded. "That would be nice."

Linda crawled back over the people at the end of the bleachers and headed back to sit with her father, who had reserved seats toward the middle of the field. Jordan apathetically watched the second half while keeping a close eye on the boys, especially J.J. Reynolds. Jordan could not quite hear their conversation, but something told her they had plans after the game. Midway through the fourth quarter, the boys became bored with the game and Brett motioned Jordan to follow him.

Brad Cooper called his mother from the ticket booth below the stadium. In a few minutes, his mother arrived in a station wagon with panel siding. Brad sat up front with his mother while Jordan sat between Brett and J.J. in the backseat. Ben Klein, who the boys called Gump, squeezed into the rear with two other boys called Peanut and Munchkin. Jordan did not know the real names of the two smaller boys, but they all fit into the station wagon for the short drive to Brad's house. Brad's mother seemed to be a nervous driver. She kept two hands on the wheel and her eyes on the road. She occasionally whispered something to her son, but seemed to be used to chauffeuring kids and ignored her passengers.

Brad Cooper lived a couple of blocks east of the Marland Mansion in a large brick house with a circle drive. Mrs. Cooper let her passengers out before parking the car in the garage and disappearing into the house. It was the end of October, but the night was pleasantly warm. Low hanging clouds pushed by a strong south breeze passed eerily over a nearly full moon.

Brad Cooper's house had a lighted patio in the back where the boys played basketball for a few minutes before J.J. Reynolds said, "This is boring. We need to do something."

"Like what?" Brett asked.

J.J. moved closer to the other boys and spoke in a soft voice. "We could go to Amanda Freely's house and toilet paper it."

"That's lame," Brett replied.

"Amanda lives right around the corner," Brad Cooper protested. "I don't want to have to deal with my parents when they see the mess in the neighborhood."

"Okay, weenies," J.J. responded. "But we need to do something. It's Halloween and not even nine o'clock yet."

"We could watch a movie on the VCR," Brad suggested.

"That's even more lame than toilet papering," J.J. sneered.

Looking around at the group of boys and Jordan, J.J. had a gleam in his eye as he said, "I know what we can do—a snipe hunt."

"A what?" Gump asked.

"A snipe hunt," J.J. repeated.

"That might work," Brett added.

"You've been snipe hunting, haven't you, B.B.?" J.J. asked.

"Sure," Brett replied. "Lots of times."

"When?" Jordan asked, whispering to her brother.

"Shut up," Brett sternly warned, as he motioned for her to be quiet.

"What's a snipe?" Brad Cooper asked.

J.J. moved closer to the other boys to speak in a soft whisper, "Snipes are a bird. Kind of like a quail or pheasant, but they're real shy and can only be caught on nights when the moon's out. You got to go deep in the woods on a moonlit night and catch them when they run for cover."

"There's no such thing," Brad Cooper protested.

"They're out there," J.J. declared. "B.B. and me went hunting last year with some guys. Winkie Dink got two!"

Brett nodded in agreement.

J.J. looked at the group of boys and said, "Ah, you guys probably aren't up to it."

"Don't listen to Coop," Ben Klein said. "I'm in. If that weirdo Winkie Dink can do it, anyone can."

"I just said I'd never heard of a snipe," Brad Cooper clarified. "And take it easy on Jody."

"Who?" Ben Klein asked in a puzzled tone.

"Winkie's name is Jody," Brad explained.

"Oh," Ben Klein shrugged.

"Don't worry about it, Coop," J.J. assured him. "You don't have to go if you're scared."

"I'm not scared of a bird!" Brad Cooper declared. "I just wanted to know what we're getting into."

"Peanut and Munchkin?" J.J. asked. "You guys as afraid as Coop."

"I'm in," Peanut declared.

"Me too," Munchkin nodded.

"I'm not afraid to go," Brad Cooper interrupted, "but I don't think we ought to be shooting up the neighborhood in the middle of the night."

J.J. Reynolds looked at Brett Bennett, and the two boys laughed.

"You don't hunt snipe with a gun," Brett explained.

"Then what do you hunt with?" Brad asked.

"You can catch 'em bare handed," J.J. claimed. "What do you think, B.B.?"

Brett looked at the other boys and said, "I don't know. It's their first time and all. Maybe we need sacks."

"What do you need sacks for?" Brad Cooper quizzed.

"You see," J.J. quickly explained. "The snipe run along the ground like a quail. B.B. and I can get into the woods and run 'em toward you. All you guys have to do is hold the sacks on the ground and call 'em. They'll come running so fast you won't see 'em until they hit the sack. There's nothing like the feeling of a snipe hitting the back of your sack, is there B.B.?"

"I've never felt anything like it," Brett agreed.

"What kind of sack do we need," an eager Ben Klein asked.

"A burlap sack works best," J.J. answered.

"We don't have any burlap sacks around here," Brad Cooper explained.

"Don't worry," J.J. responded. "You got some pillow cases in the house, don't you?"

"Sure," a wary Brad replied.

"Go get 'em," J.J. ordered. "Unless, of course, you're chicken."

"I told you I'm not afraid to go to the woods in the dark," Brad claimed. "I've been huntin' plenty of times with my dad. I just wanted to know what to expect."

"Now you know," J.J. said. "Can you find us some sacks?"

Brad Cooper nodded and headed into the house.

"Grab a flashlight when you're in there," J.J. said as Brad walked away.

The other boys anxiously asked a barrage of questions while Brad went into the house. They ignored Jordan, who listened silently on the edge of their conversation. Brad returned in a few minutes with pillow cases bulging from under his dark sweatshirt. He handed each boy a soft, white pillow case before handing the last one to Jordan.

"She's not going," Brett protested.

"Oh, come on, B.B.," J.J. interjected. "JorDAN will be okay. If it's safe enough for Coop, your kid sister will be fine."

Brett looked unconvinced but nodded in agreement. The group led by J.J. walked through the dark neighborhood toward the Marland Mansion. Brad Cooper's house was less than two blocks away. They crawled underneath a section of wrought iron guarding a drainage spout in the stone wall. It was not quite 10 o'clock when the group got to the edge of the woods, but it felt like midnight to Jordan.

"From now on, we got to be quiet," J.J. explained. "We don't want to scare off any snipe and there's a crazy old woman that lives out in these woods."

"Is it the old woman with the cat that hangs out around here?" Jordan asked.

J.J. did not pay the girl much attention, but replied, "Probably. Now everyone stay close and no talking. When I find a good area, I'll tell you what to do."

The group headed into the dark woods. It was Halloween night, but a warm southern breeze rustled through the brown, lifeless leaves still clinging to the trees. Some of the leaves had already let go for autumn and there was a muffled crunch as the group followed J.J. along a narrow trail. Jordan's heart raced with the excitement of the hunt. Although J.J. had told the boys to be silent, they continued to poke at each other and try to get the others to break their silence. J.J. motioned them to be quiet several times, but he relentlessly led them deeper into the thick woods. The group reached an old fence with a "NO TRESPASSING" sign attached. J.J. ignored the warning and led them over the fence. When Brad Cooper tried to protest, J.J. motioned him to be silent. J.J. signaled the group to stop about a hundred yards past the fence in an opening in the trees.

The group huddled close to him as J.J. said, "We're getting real close. Turn the flashlight off to get your eyes adjusted to the moonlight, but be careful to the left. The pits are close and I don't want to have to haul one of you guys out. Don't panic when you hear the snipe coming. You'll want to run and maybe scream, but hold your ground. B.B. and I will chase the snipe right to you."

"How will we know they're coming?" Ben Klein asked.

"Don't worry about that," J.J. assured him. "Just keep the position and make your call. You'll know when you have one."

"What call?" Brad Cooper asked.

J.J. looked at Brett and said, "Show 'em, B.B.."

Brett looked at J.J. with a hint of aggravation, and said, "Cup your hands close to your mouth and shout 'Kaw-Kaw...Whoop...Whoop!'"

The group timidly replied, "Kaw-Kaw...Whoop...Whoop."

"Louder," J.J. insisted. "The snipe won't come running for a wimpy call like that."

"Kaw-Kaw...Whoop...Whoop!" the group repeated.

"Louder!" J.J. coached.

"Kaw-Kaw...Whoop...Whoop!" they shouted.

"Good!" J.J. smiled. "We'll get snipe for sure tonight. Now B.B. and I will go a little farther out in the woods and drive the snipe to this opening. You guys keep making the call and the snipe will come running. Let me have the flashlights."

"What do you need the flashlights for?" Brad asked.

J.J. thought for a moment and answered, "B.B. and I have to get pretty far back into the woods. Snipe hate the light and if one of you guys gets scared and turns on a light you'll blow the whole deal."

Before the group could ask more questions, J.J. and Brett walked into the dark woods and disappeared in the dense foliage.

"Make the call!" J.J. shouted, when he and Brett were out of sight.

"Kaw-Kaw...Whoop...Whoop!" the group shouted a few times in the dark night.

"There's no such thing as a snipe," Brad Cooper factually deduced after a few minutes.

"Sure there is," an anxious Ben Klein assured him. "Keep your bag down and be ready."

Brad Cooper straightened up and said, "I'm telling you, they're pulling a trick on us. They're going to circle around to scare us or leave us out here in the dark. I bet they're laughing at us now."

"There's snipe in these woods," an anxious Munchkin declared as he hunched nervously close to the ground. "I've heard my big brother talk about 'em."

"Kaw-Kaw...Whoop...Whoop!" the small boy shouted urgently.

After a few more calls, the boy called Peanut stood up and said, "I think Coop's right, guys. We've been had."

"No way!" Ben Klein protested. "Those guys wouldn't do that. They know I'd crush them."

"Kaw-Kaw...Whoop...Whoop!" Ben Klein loudly shouted.

"Come on, Gump," Brad Cooper pleaded. "The longer we stay out here the bigger fools we are."

"I tell you, I'm going to catch one," Ben Klein insisted.

"I saw something!" Munchkin excitedly shouted.

The group was silent for a moment, before a distinctive rustling was heard deep in the dark woods.

"I saw one!" Munchkin claimed. "They're coming!"

Peanut resumed his position while shouting timid snipe calls. Brad Cooper looked into the woods where there was a distinct sound that was not natural coming their way.

"Told you!" an excited Ben Klein shouted.

A loud, "Bam! Bam!" ripped through the night.

"That's a gunshot!" Brad Cooper screamed.

A second later the panicked voices of J.J. Reynolds and Brett shouted, "Run!"

Two dots of light moved quickly through the woods.

"I told you they were trying to scare us," Brad Cooper nervously proclaimed.

Two more blasts from a shotgun ripped through the night, followed by Brett and J.J. streaking past the group.

"Run!" Brett screamed. "She's crazy! I'm not fooling!"

The two didn't slow down as they ran recklessly through the thick woods. The other boys looked at each other a second before running after them. Jordan, however, froze in fear. She wanted to run with the boys more than anything, but she could not make her legs move. In a moment, she stood alone in the quiet, lonely woods.

Jordan had about regained her ability to breathe normally when she heard an ominous rustling sound coming from deeper in the woods. She had been unsure about the existence of snipe in the woods, but she could not ignore the fact that something big was coming toward her. In the darkness, Jordan could see an ominous form moving through the trees.

"What are you doing here?" an angry female voice shouted from the darkness.

A stout woman of about fifty with a shotgun cradled in her arms stepped into the small clearing and glared fiercely at the young girl.

"I—I," Jordan stuttered.

"This is my property!" the woman shouted. "I don't want any of you snot-nosed kids trespassing!"

Jordan tried to nod, but before she could react, the woman said, "Now git!" as she fired her gun harmlessly into the air.

Jordan sprinted away into the dark woods. Her heart pounded and she was sure she would be shot as soon as the woman could reload. Jordan continued to run until she worked up the courage to look back. Behind her was nothing but darkness and empty forest. An instant before Jordan slowed down, she felt the earth move from under her feet and fell shoulder first into a pit. She looked up at the canopy of trees above her and wondered if she were dead or alive.

CHAPTER 19

Jordan gasped for air as she struggled to gain her bearings. She had fallen into a pit with about six inches of water in it. Although muddy, Jordan was not hurt except for having the breath knocked out of her. She stood up to see if the crazy woman with the shotgun still hunted her. Jordan was cautious at first, but panicked when she realized she could not see over the edge of the pit. She was trapped in a square pit about eight feet square and deeper than her head. She tried several times to jump and get a grip on the edge, but failed each time. The faint whine of sirens howled in the distance, and she imagined that someone was coming to rescue her. The sirens, however, never got close and soon the sound faded away.

Exhausted from her many tries at escape, Jordan finally fell to her knees in the six inches of muddy water in the bottom of the pit and did the only thing she could think of doing—cry. Jordan had seen the boys run. She should have run too. They would be stupid to come back into the woods at night with a crazy woman with a shotgun lurking there. She was trapped.

Jordan wiped her face with her muddy hands and looked up at the moonlight creeping through the broken clouds above. She regained some composure and began to feel safe in the pit. J.J. had warned the group about the existence of the rugged terrain and the pits, but the disoriented Jordan had run the wrong way. She was tired, wet, and although the night was not cold, Jordan was uncomfortably chilly.

I can survive, Jordan thought to herself.

It was getting late. She did not know the time, but figured she must have been in the pit half an hour and it must be close to eleven. Her mother would be home at midnight. Jordan was facing grounding, maybe more. Jordan could imagine that reform school might be on her mother's mind after this incident.

A miserable Jordan had about given up when she heard a loud whisper in the night calling, "Jordan!"

The voice was familiar, but the tone was not. Jordan was so used to the mocking, "JorDAN," that she did not immediately recognize the confident voice of J.J. Reynolds.

"Down here!" an exuberant Jordan shouted.

"Keep it down," J.J. Reynolds whispered, as he peered over the edge of the pit that had trapped Jordan. "You all right?"

"I think so," Jordan replied.

"Can you reach my hand?" J.J. asked as he reached down.

Jordan was easily able to grasp J.J.'s wrist and he effortlessly pulled her out of the pit. Jordan nearly fell into his arms, but he gently pushed her away.

"You're a mess," J.J. said with a smirk.

Mud and dirt covered Jordan from her shoes to her hair.

"Sorry," Jordan muttered.

J.J. let out a half-laugh and replied, "I'm just glad to find you. Let's get out of here."

He took Jordan's hand and pulled her quickly through the dense woods. Jordan was disoriented, but occasionally got a glimpse of the moon above.

Almost out of desperation, Jordan asked, "Did we get any snipes?"

J.J. good-naturedly chuckled and said, "Not tonight."

In a few minutes, J.J. and Jordan arrived at the opening next to the Marland Mansion. Peanut and Munchkin sprinted into the woods to find Brett and Brad Cooper and in a few minutes they emerged from the forest and ran toward Jordan.

"Are you okay?" Brett asked.

Jordan nodded, as J.J. answered, "She slipped into one of the pits, but she's fine except for the mud."

"You look like you took a mud bath," Brett observed.

Jordan tried to shake some of the muck off, but had little success.

"Take this," Brad Cooper offered as he tossed one of the pillow cases the boys had carried into the woods toward Jordan.

"Thanks," a cavalier J.J. Reynolds said as he intercepted the pillow case and wiped his hands before handing it to Jordan.

Jordan tried to wipe some of the mud from her face, but the pillow case quickly became a muddy mess.

"We better get you cleaned up before Mom gets home," Brett suggested.

Jordan nodded obediently and took a step to follow Brett. The boys chattered with nervous energy after finding Jordan. The shotgun blasts had caught the attention of the local police and the boys had been playing hide and seek with the officers while trying to find Jordan. They found out later they had wandered onto the back edge of the Ford place. Mrs. Ford was an eccentric old farmer's wife who had fired her shotgun in the air more than a few times. For years the farm had been on the outskirts of town and Mrs. Ford had not become accustomed to her place being so close to town. On Halloween night, she had been vigilant about protecting her rundown property from any tricks or treats.

Jordan was content to let the boys brag about their imagined heroics and followed diligently behind as they approached the great Marland house with moonlight illuminating its rock walls. To the back of the house, Jordan caught a glimpse of an image that seemed to glow against the dark. She was not frightened and immediately recognized the stooped silhouette of Lydie Marland.

"Do you see her?" Jordan excitedly asked.

The surprised boys hushed their banter to turn and look at Jordan.

"Over there!" Jordan pointed.

The boys turned to look, but a disappointed Jordan could see the woman had disappeared into the shadows.

"If you're trying to scare us, it's not going to work," J.J. Reynolds cynically responded.

"No," Jordan protested. "I'm not trying to scare you. The old woman I'm always telling you about was at the back of the house."

"I don't see anyone," Brett said.

"I know," Jordan sighed, "but she was there. I promise I'm not seeing things."

"So this invisible woman you keep telling us about," J.J. started with a smirk, "was there, but has—disappeared."

"Lay off," Brad Cooper interrupted. "I've seen the old woman around. You have too—you just don't pay attention."

Brett sighed and said, "I don't see anything, but an old cat."

Jordan squinted into the darkness a moment before spotting the cat prowling in the shadows.

"That's her cat!" Jordan replied, before heading toward the back of the house.

The boys followed as Jordan quickly approached the cat. As Jordan got close, the cat darted away toward the boathouse to the north of the mansion. Jordan steadily followed as the boys tagged along behind.

The cat darted into the darkness of the three arches at the boathouse and Jordan whispered, "Here kitty, kitty…here kitty, kitty."

"What are you doing?" an impatient Brett asked as he stepped under the three arches.

"The cat came in here," Jordan explained. "The cat belongs to the old woman—her name is Lydie."

"The cat?" Brett asked.

"No, the woman," Jordan explained.

The group stood silently in the dark confines of the boathouse when a low pitched moan seemed to reverberate from the ground.

"What was that?" J.J. asked.

"I don't know!" Ben Klein nervously replied.

As the group stared at a dark hole in the wall, the moan came again.

"Let's get out of here," J.J. Reynolds meekly suggested.

Before the group could take a step, however, a bright light glared from behind them and they all screamed in the dark night.

CHAPTER 20

"What are you doing here?" the authoritarian voice asked from behind a bright light.

The speechless group of kids stared blankly at the uniformed security guard questioning them.

"We were heading home," Brett finally explained. "My sister thought she saw a cat come in here."

The security officer flashed his light around the empty space until it stopped on the open door leading to the dark tunnel. He was a thin, nervous-looking man in his early thirties. His uniform fit poorly and he had a holster that held his radio and flashlight instead of a firearm. A deep, moaning howl of air moving out of the tunnel made a soft yet eerie sound.

"Were you kids breaking in?" the security officer charged.

"No!" they answered in unison.

When the security officer reached for his radio, Brad said, "We weren't trying to break in, Russell."

The security officer shined the light in Brad's face and said, "You're the Cooper kid, right?"

"Yes, sir," Brad answered. "I live a couple of blocks away."

The security officer studied the group of kids for a moment before shining his light into the darkness of the tunnel. The breeze moaned through the long, dark tunnel.

"Where does it go?" J.J. Reynolds brashly asked.

"Never you mind," the security officer answered.

Brett pointed at the door and said, "Look, it's unlocked. We weren't trying to break in. Someone left it open. We wouldn't have gone in."

The security officer examined the door with the padlock hanging limply on the latch.

Turning to the group of kids he said, "Everyone empty your pockets."

The group complied and soon an assortment of pocket paraphernalia including loose change, keys, chewing gum, and a rabbit's foot appeared. The security officer quickly tried all the keys, but it was soon evident none fit the large padlock. The security guard shined his light down the dark tunnel as the group watched in silence. Deep in the darkness the faint patter of steps could be heard.

"Someone's in there," Brett whispered.

"Do you know who it is?" the security officer asked.

"We just got here," Brett explained. "Maybe it's a ghost."

"Are you going after them?" J.J. Reynolds smirked.

The security officer swallowed hard and said, "My first job is to secure the property. It's nearly eleven o'clock. You kids need to get home."

None of the group hesitated at the opportunity to leave as the security officer shut the massive door and tested the lock. Everyone said a quick good bye before heading their separate ways. J.J. Reynolds walked with Jordan and Brett since he lived in their direction. By the time they passed the iron gate, J.J. was buzzing with theories about ghosts and whispers in the night. Jordan turned back to look at the dark house, wondering if the old woman had sneaked inside.

She did not have to wonder long. Jordan caught a glimpse of the cat darting toward the small stone house along the rock wall and saw Lydie standing in the shadows. Jordan did not interrupt J.J.'s bold talk, as she walked silently behind the boys.

When she got home, Jordan took a quick bath and changed into clean pajamas while Brett washed her muddy clothes. By the time her mother came home from work, Jordan rested peacefully in her soft, safe bed.

CHAPTER 21

November blew in with a cold chill, and Jordan discovered her coat from the previous year fit tightly. Jordan reluctantly wore her out-of-style jacket to school only on the coldest days. Other times, she braved frigid temperatures rather than the judgments of her classmates about her fashion sense.

School days were long and uneventful for Jordan. She did not fit in with any of the junior high groups. Linda Pelletier became a regular lunch buddy, and Jordan began to appreciate the girl's quick wit and sense of irony.

Thanksgiving break should have been a relief from the drudgery of school, but Jordan knew this holiday would be different. Her mother purchased a small pre-cooked turkey from the Safeway store and Jordan's family ate their lunch while her father celebrated with his new family. Jordan actually felt sorry for her mother, who tried so desperately to put on a brave face for her children. The holiday also provided an opportunity for Barbara Bennett to get overtime pay at the hospital filling in as a receptionist. By early afternoon, Jordan and Brett were home alone.

"What are you doing?" Jordan asked as her brother Brett tied his tennis shoes and put on a heavy sweatshirt.

"I'm playing football," Brett explained. "Coop's family has a game each Thanksgiving and he invited me to play."

Jordan had not seen Brad Cooper in many weeks. Brad had been grounded by his mother for ruining her Egyptian cotton pillow cases during their now infamous Halloween snipe hunt.

"Can I come?" Jordan pleaded.

Brett frowned and looked around the empty house before saying, "Sure."

The brother and sister walked silently up Monument Road toward the Marland Mansion. Brett had been sullen and brooding since the man had come to collect the rent. Jordan had noticed that his old group of friends did not come to their house as much. Brad Cooper seemed to be the only friend that had stuck close. His family lived a couple of blocks from the mansion and the game would be played in the large lawn behind the mansion.

It was nearly two o'clock when Jordan spotted Brad Cooper tossing a football to a smaller boy wearing a crimson jersey. The Cooper family had an odd assortment of players assembled for their game, from young boys to middle aged men. Brad Cooper waved enthusiastically at a timid Brett to join him. Brett glanced at his sister before heading down the slight slope to the lawn. Jordan stayed behind and leaned against the railing of the walkway that went over the boathouse below.

Jordan watched with bittersweet melancholy as the Cooper family organized for the game. It reminded her of some of the holidays she had shared with her father's family in past years. Her family was never as sports-crazy as the group she watched this afternoon, but they had been a family and their gathering had been a place to go for the holidays.

The teams had been selected and the game was about to begin when Brad Cooper trotted across the lawn toward the raised spot from which Jordan was watching.

"You can play, too," Brad offered, as Jordan looked down at him.

Jordan looked around to see that she would be the only girl and replied, "I'd rather watch."

Brad smiled and said, "Come on down if you change your mind."

As Brad ran back to the group, Jordan wondered if she should have agreed to play. As she looked at the other players, Jordan determined that besides Brad, Brett, and a few other teenage boys, she would have been athletic enough to have played. It was not cold, but a cool breeze went through her thin sweatshirt and some exercise would have kept her warm.

"That young man pays you a lot of attention," a voice from behind her spoke.

Jordan turned around to see Lydie walking up behind her following her cat. The cat rubbed up against Jordan and the girl reached down and gently stroked its back. The cat quickly tired of the attention and retreated back toward the old woman.

The old woman continued, "I can't tell who likes you more—the cat or that young man."

"I don't think either likes me that much," a flustered Jordan replied.

The old woman walked up to Jordan and surveyed the grounds and the football game that was beginning. Jordan knew the old woman was protective of the property, but after a thoughtful inspection she seemed happy to see people enjoying the field.

Without looking at Jordan, Lydie said, "I wouldn't be so sure. I don't think the young man needs you down there for your athletic abilities."

"My brother's playing," Jordan nervously stated, anxious to change the subject.

"I never really understood football," the woman confessed. "I guess it does make more sense than baseball, though."

"Did you have a good Thanksgiving?" Jordan asked.

The old woman appeared aggravated at the question and replied, "It's just another day to an old woman."

"Yeah," Jordan sighed. "Holidays are the pits."

The old woman studied the young girl for a moment before saying, "That doesn't seem like a healthy attitude for someone your age."

"I'm sorry," Jordan apologized. "It's just—"

Jordan did not finish her thought and decided not to bore the old woman with her family problems.

"No need to apologize," Lydie assured her, "or to explain."

"It's just that this is the first Thanksgiving without my father," Jordan admitted.

"I'm sorry," Lydie said. "Did he pass this year?"

It took Jordan a second to understand what the old woman was asking before she replied, "No, he's fine. My parents divorced this year."

"Oh," she sighed. "I forgot that's how things are done these days. When I was younger, divorce was seen as quite a scandal, but times have changed."

"Not for the better," Jordan fumed.

"I'm tired," the old woman sighed. "Let's sit in the gazebo. You can still see the game from there."

Jordan followed Lydie to a small octagonal structure with a stone floor, red tile roof, and benches. The small shelter overlooked the lawn where the Cooper family played football. Jordan sat across from Lydie and noticed how feeble and frail she looked. Lydie seemed tired, but she had an air of contentment as she enjoyed the autumn afternoon.

"We won't have this pleasant weather much longer," Lydie lamented.

Jordan desperately searched for something to say. She felt trapped in the gazebo having to sit face to face with the old woman. When Jordan looked away in frustration, Lydie's cat jumped in her lap and began licking her hands.

"There kitty," Jordon coaxed, as she petted the skinny cat.

"Get off her," the old woman scolded the cat.

"She's fine," Jordan smiled.

"Silly cat," Lydie sighed. "She likes you. That cat doesn't like many people. You must have had turkey for lunch. I haven't eaten meat in years. I couldn't now if I wanted with these worn teeth of mine."

"She's bony," Jordan observed, as she gently rubbed behind the cat's ears. "What's that mark above her eye?"

"This cat's had a hard life," the woman explained. "She's lost more fights than she's won, but I keep her fed now."

Jordan listened as the woman continued, "This cat was born on a farm with four brothers: Cairo, Sydney, Chicago, and Dallas."

"I remember you telling me she was named after the city in Italy," Jordan recalled.

"Yes," Lydie nodded. "All the kittens were named after great cities. As kittens they all fought and played as poor farm cats are apt to do."

Lydie frowned as she continued, "One day, a woman from town came to the farm. She lived in a big house in town, but she had seen a mouse and determined that she needed a cat to keep the mice away. The woman did not particularly like the looks of her, but the cat was not as wild as her brothers, so the woman brought her home.

"This cat is not impressive-looking, but she's a sweet cat and the woman soon grew very fond of her. When the weather turned cold or wet, the woman would let her come inside. The cat entertained the woman so much, that she soon became a house cat.

"The woman took the cat to the vet regularly, had her declawed so she couldn't damage the expensive furniture, and even bought a fat velvet pillow for the cat to nap on. This cat had the best of everything and was treated like a princess, while her brothers survived hunting mice, rats, and squirrels in the barn on the farm.

"The cat walked around the house like she owned the place and did whatever she wanted in between her lengthy naps. Her life was a dream until the old woman died one day. The family prepared the house to be sold and put the cat outside. They didn't have the heart to take her to a shelter were she would surely have been put out of her misery. After a while, everyone forgot about the cat that had been a princess and the cat was on her own."

"Cats are resilient," Lydie explained. "This cat was forced to fend for herself. She had gone too far from home and her brothers would not have understood her inability to hunt. She stayed in the neighborhood and scavenged through the garbage cans trying to survive. The neighbors called animal control and that's when the cat and I met. She had been in a fight with a tomcat and had scratches on her little face. The animal control man wanted to take her. I knew he would put her down, but all she had tried to do was survive. It wasn't her fault that she didn't really know how."

"That's terrible," Jordan frowned.

"That's why the cat stays close to me," Lydie proclaimed. "I told the man she was my cat and to let her be. I found I still had some influence in this town because he let us alone. We've been together ever since. We're both a little bony, but we have each other now."

Jordan took greater care in holding the cat after hearing of her past struggles.

"She is a sweet cat," Jordan smiled.

Lydie nodded, "She's very suspicious. She won't let many people hold her."

Jordan continued to cuddle the cat as Lydie looked around the mansion grounds.

"The leaves are about gone," Lydie complained. "We'll have four months of cold, dark days until spring shines on the palace again."

Jordan watched as sadness seemed to overtake the old woman.

"We need to get home, cat," Lydie finally determined.

She pulled herself up from the bench before Jordan could assist her and started walking away from the gazebo. Her cat instinctively jumped to the ground and followed the old woman.

After a few steps, Lydie turned around to say, "Have a happy holiday and enjoy watching your game."

Jordan acknowledged the old woman with a nod before Lydie and the cat walked to the north. Jordan watched the two for a few minutes and saw Lydie enter a small house that sat on the mansion grounds inside the fence surrounded by a large brick patio.

"So that's where she lives," Jordan whispered to herself.

Jordan walked back to a spot overlooking the lawn and the Coopers' football game. She thought about the old woman who had observed the surrounding hints of winter to come. The game ended before dark and Jordan walked silently, but contently with Brett back to her world in their little rent house on 13th Street.

CHAPTER 22

"How was it?" Linda Pelletier cautiously asked in the school lunch room after the Christmas break.

Jordan sighed noticeably and replied, "Awkward. Even seeing Chloe was weird. Her mom tried to act cool, but she couldn't look me in the eye. Brett came, but he was determined to show Dad how miserable he was."

"Sounds tough," Linda said.

Jordan nodded and asked, "How was your holiday?"

"Fine," Linda shrugged. "The same old same old."

The two girls finished lunch, glad to be back in the routine of school. Jordan enjoyed Linda's quirky humor and off-beat perspective about school life. Linda helped make Jordan's crumbling family situation bearable.

The school day had been uneventful and Jordan sprinted from the bus to avoid the chilly north wind on a January afternoon. Jordan was surprised to see her mother's car parked in the driveway. Her mother was rarely home in the afternoons and Jordan cautiously opened the front door.

"Hey, Jordan," her mother cheerfully greeted her.

"Hi," Jordan replied. "What are you doing home?"

"I had a few minutes before my clinicals this afternoon and brought something for my favorite daughter," Barbara Bennett smiled.

"Do you have more than one daughter?" Jordan cynically replied.

"No silly," Barbara responded. "I found you a coat."

Jordan looked at a waist-length blue coat her mother handed to her.

"Did you get this from the Salvation Army?" Jordan asked.

Barbara looked disappointed as she replied, "No, I found it on sale."

Jordan could tell she had hurt her mother's feelings with her question and sheepishly added, "I was kidding. It's nice and I really need it. Thanks, Mom."

"You're welcome," Barbara sighed.

Jordan stepped to her mother and was surprised to have her mother hold her so tightly.

"This may be the end of an era," Barbara smiled, as she let go of her daughter. "You're probably going to buy your own clothes from now on."

"What?" a puzzled Jordan asked.

"I have a surprise for you," Barbara explained. "I've found you an afternoon job where you can make some spending money."

"Where?" Jordan quizzed.

"Mr. Grumman was at the hospital the other day," Barbara explained. "I had a nice conversation with him and he was telling me he could use some help with housekeeping and a few odd chores."

"Mr. Grumpy!" Jordan exclaimed. "You want to send me to Mr. Grumpy to work!"

"Don't call him that," Barbara scolded. "He's a nice man and needs some help."

"Mom," Jordan protested. "Everyone in the neighborhood knows he's a creepy old man. Everyone has warned us kids to stay away from Grumpy Old Man's Corner, since we moved here."

"Who?" Barbara asked.

"Everyone," Jordan claimed. "All of Brett's friends anyway."

"Including J.J. Reynolds?" Barbara quizzed.

Jordan nodded, as she endured her mother's judgmental stare.

"He's just particular about his place," Barbara explained.

"What about us ruining his yard?" Jordan added. "Did you ever think he's figured out we butchered his yard and now he'll want to butcher me?"

"Don't be silly," Barbara sighed. "I told Mr. Grumman what happened a few days after he returned home. He appreciated the effort."

"What's going on?" Brett asked, as he emerged from his room.

"Mom's trying to get me killed!" Jordan replied. "She wants me to work at Mr. Grumman's house."

"Jordan, don't be so dramatic," Barbara Bennett scolded. "Mr. Grumman needs some help and I thought you might want to earn a little money. I won't make you do anything, but you know I wouldn't put you anywhere that wasn't safe. He says he'll pay twenty dollars a week and all you have to do is go twice a week to vacuum and dust."

"I'd do it," Brett declared.

"Really?" an unconvinced Jordan asked.

"Sure," Brett answered. "That's more per hour than I make busting boxes at TG&Y. How dirty could Mr. Grumpy be?"

"Stop calling him that!" Barbara Bennett warned.

"Sorry," Brett shrugged. "Go for it, Jordan. If you don't show up in a couple of days, we'll go digging in his backyard looking for your body parts."

"Brett, you're not helping," Barbara stated.

"I'm teasing," Brett smiled. "It'll be easy money, Sis."

Jordan studied her brother for a moment to determine his sincerity before asking, "It's only two days a week?"

"Just a couple of hours two days a week," Barbara assured her. "You don't have to do it, but it might be nice having money of your own."

Jordan thought for a moment and said, "I'll do it."

"Good," Barbara sighed. "I already told Mr. Grumman you'd be glad to. He's expecting you tomorrow after school."

Jordan looked warily at her mother before turning to Brett. "Don't tell any of your friends I'm working for Mr. Grumman; they'll never let me hear the end of it."

"I won't," Brett nodded.

"And if I don't come home," Jordan sighed. "Come look for me."

CHAPTER 23

"Got your report done?" a chipper Linda Pelletier asked as she took the seat next to Jordan.

"Where were you yesterday?" Jordan asked.

Linda covered her smile with a frown and said, "I was at the dentist getting these stupid braces tightened."

"Do they hurt?" Jordan asked.

"A little," Linda shrugged. "I get used to them and then the dentist will do his best to make me uncomfortable by tightening them up."

"They don't look that bad, you know?" Jordan offered.

Linda looked suspiciously at her friend and replied, "They don't look that good, either."

Jordan laughed and Linda continued, "The dentist says I'll have them off by my sophomore year. It's not like I have that much of a life now."

"You'll be beautiful, and I'll still be a social outcast," Jordan lamented.

Linda shook her head and said, "If I had your smile, I wouldn't complain. You just got to learn to use it. You didn't answer the question. Did you do your report?"

"Not yet," Jordan confessed. "I'm not finding motivation."

Jordan's English teacher had assigned a five page theme paper due in another week. Jordan had started a dozen times scribbling notes, but had yet to pick a concrete topic for the paper.

"You better get inspired," Linda coached. "It's due next Friday."

"I know," Jordan sighed. "What are you doing yours on?"

"I'm writing on Greta Garbo," Linda explained. "There's a book in the library about old movie stars and I saw her picture. She's famous for saying, 'I want to be alone.'"

"I can get that," Jordan smiled. "I wish people would leave me alone—and I wish they'd include me sometimes."

"You are complex," Linda teased.

"Why don't you come to the library with me this afternoon?" Linda asked.

"Downtown?" Jordan clarified.

"Sure," Linda explained. "Mom'll take us."

"I don't think your mom will be too anxious to take me anywhere after our last trip," Jordan observed.

"Mom's over that," Linda declared. "Besides, how lost could you get in Ponca?"

Jordan frowned and said, "I'd like to go, but not today."

"Why not?" Linda asked.

"My mother's found me gainful employment," Jordan explained.

"You got a job?"

"Kinda."

"Where?"

"I'm cleaning Mr. Grumman's house," Jordan explained. "He's paying me ten dollars a day."

"Ten dollars!" Linda smiled. "To go to Mr. Grumpy's house?"

"You know him?" a concerned Jordan asked.

Linda nodded as she sipped her milk.

"Do you think—" Jordan cautiously asked. "Do you think I'll be okay?"

"Sure," Linda replied. "He's called Mr. Grumpy, not Mr. Dangerous or Mr. Ax Murderer."

"What do you know about him?" Jordan asked. "Why do they call him Mr. Grumpy?"

"Because he's grumpy," Linda answered.

"I know that," Jordan fumed.

"My dad says he's a CAVE man," Linda shared.

"CAVE man?" a confused Jordan replied.

"Citizen Against Virtually Everything," Linda explained. "He's always writing letters to the editor complaining about—

everything. He got after the band a few years ago for practicing so early in the morning and 'disturbing the peace.'"

"He sounds crazy," Jordan said.

"Not crazy, grumpy," Linda smiled. "You'll be fine—just don't mess up any of his stuff. He's real particular about his stuff."

"Great," Jordan sighed. "I really wish I could go to the library with you now."

"I'd rather have the ten bucks," Linda encouraged her.

The school day ended and Jordan enjoyed the warmth of her coat as she boarded the school bus. Her feelings of dread increased, however, as the bus approached 13th Street. Twenty dollars a week sounded great, but she would first have to endure Mr. Grumman. Jordan left a note for her brother Brett to look for her if she wasn't back by five o'clock.

As Jordan approached the front door, she noticed the zebra-like striping adorning Mr. Grumman's front yard where Brett had scalped it. The cool weather came before the lawn grew back, leaving a scar that would last until spring. Jordan knocked on the door softly and heard nothing from inside the house. She almost went home to explain to her mother that she had tried to do the chores, but no one was home. After a moment, she knocked harder and soon heard ominous shuffling from inside. The door creaked open and Jordan could feel the warm stale air from inside.

Mr. Grumman peeked out from behind the door and stated flatly, "You're here."

With no further greeting, he swung the door open to let Jordan enter. A silent Jordan stepped meekly inside and heard the door slam shut behind her. In the dim lighting, Jordan was somewhat relieved to see the front room was fairly neat.

"My mother said you needed some housecleaning?" Jordan asked.

"Yes," Mr. Grumman mumbled. "I met your mother a few days ago at the hospital and told her I needed someone."

"Where would you like me to start?" Jordan asked.

Mr. Grumman looked around as if confused as to how to give directions and said, "Why don't you start in the kitchen and we'll see how that goes."

Jordan nodded and located the small kitchen close to the front room. She was relieved Mr. Grumman retreated to his chair to read. Jordan needed to ask where he kept the cleaning supplies, but decided to prowl around on her own. If Mr. Grumman was content to leave her alone, she could manage. Jordan found a tub with cleaner and supplies underneath the kitchen sink and began wiping the countertops. The kitchen was fairly clean except for several dishes piled in the sink. After cleaning the countertops and small table, Jordan turned on the water to start washing the dishes.

"What are you doing?" Mr. Grumman barked from the front room.

Before Jordan could reply, she heard him rising up from his chair.

"I'm washing the dishes," Jordan replied nervously.

Mr. Grumman soon appeared at the door to the kitchen to scowl at his young helper.

"That's not necessary," he explained. "I have a dishwasher beside the sink. Just stick the dishes in there."

An uncomfortable silence followed, as Jordan anxiously began putting plates and glasses into the dishwasher.

Mr. Grumman seemed to realize he was making the girl uncomfortable when he said, "I'm not used to giving instructions—I've always been able to manage things on my own."

"I'm fine," Jordan assured him, as she continued to work.

Mr. Grumman watched her working feverishly for a moment and said, "I'll leave you to your work. Ask if you need anything."

Jordan nodded and continued cleaning as she heard the man's steps retreat back to the front room. Jordan could not imagine a situation where she would purposely interrupt Mr. Grumman. Jordan looked out the window of the kitchen into Mr. Grumman's backyard. His backyard was guarded by a high wood fence. Jordan had never seen the yard, but it was neatly trimmed with several white rocks lined up like tombstones along the fence.

In a few minutes, Jordan softly stated, "I'm finished in the kitchen."

Mr. Grumman pulled himself up from the chair as Jordan waited in tense silence for her instructions. He walked slowly past Jordan and into the kitchen to survey the work.

Seeing the blinds were open exposing his backyard, Mr. Grumman moved to block the view and hide his tombstones in the back.

"You do thorough work," he finally smiled, when it was clear Jordan would not ask questions about his peculiar yard art.

"Thank you," Jordan replied. "What would you like me to do next?"

Mr. Grumman looked around as if confused by the question and said, "I guess you could dust and vacuum the front room and bedrooms."

Jordan nodded politely and asked, "Where do you keep the vacuum cleaner?"

Mr. Grumman led her to a small closet where a heavy, antique-looking machine greeted her.

"I'll read the paper in the kitchen," Mr. Grumman offered as Jordan wrestled the vacuum out of the closet.

She quickly dusted the few pieces of furnishings in the front room before running the vacuum cleaner over the avocado-green carpeting. The aluminum foil Mr. Grumman kept on the windows made it difficult for Jordan to see in the dim light. After finishing the front room, she quickly moved to a bedroom that she assumed was Mr. Grumman's. A pair of trousers hanging on the closet door was the only thing even remotely out of place. She quickly dusted and swept the room.

Jordan finished every room except for a small bedroom in the back of the house.

She cautiously opened the door and muffled her gasp at what faced her. A folding table stood cluttered in the middle of the room. The walls were covered with bookcases that were so full Jordan imagined that they might cave in on her. She was about to ask for instructions on how to tackle this room when something caused her to stop. Jordan stepped toward a bookcase with old pictures seemingly piled randomly into it.

A picture on top of the pile caught Jordan's attention. It was an old black and white photograph of young adults dressed in costumes. A playbill leaned next to the photograph, but Jordan focused on the picture. If she had not seen the painting in the mansion, Jordan would not have recognized Lydie Marland dressed as Juliet sitting with about a dozen other people. The girl in the picture had a calm sadness to her, which was not detectable in the painting.

"You don't have to clean in here," Mr. Grumman interrupted her.

He stepped into the room and took the picture from Jordan. His voice was composed, but his body language said he was not comfortable with a visitor in his cluttered room.

"I haven't," Jordan awkwardly replied. "I mean I haven't cleaned in here yet."

Mr. Grumman looked nervously around the small room as if taking inventory and said apologetically, "This is my memories room. I know it's a mess, but I can find things the way they are. I do some historical research for the county historical society."

Jordan unconsciously looked at the photograph Mr. Grumman held carefully in his hand.

"You must think this old picture is quite amusing," Mr. Grumman stiffly noted. "It was a long time ago."

"What year was it taken?" Jordan asked.

Mr. Grumman looked at the picture and replied, "The photograph was taken in 1918, during the war. I played Friar Lawrence in a Shakespearean theater that summer."

"May I look?" Jordan asked.

Mr. Grumman was surprised at the interest, but he handed her the picture.

"Where's this taken?" Jordan asked.

"The Marland home," Mr. Grumman answered. "It was on the veranda overlooking the gardens."

"Not the mansion on the hill?" Jordan clarified as she studied the photograph.

"No," Mr. Grumman said, "the house on Grand."

Jordon looked at the picture a moment longer before she was able to recognize a younger Mr. Grumman. He did not look natural. His stern stare and perpetual scowl were replaced by an innocent smirk, as if he were planning some great prank on the others.

"This is Lydie?" Jordan asked.

Mr. Grumman studied the young girl for a moment and pointed at the picture to say, "Yes. She was in a lot of our plays back then. I'm surprised you recognized her. There aren't that many pictures of a young Lydie Marland around town."

"I saw a painting of her in the mansion," Jordan replied. "I wouldn't have recognized her otherwise. She looks happy and sad at the same time in this picture."

Mr. Grumman took the picture back from Jordan to study it more carefully.

"I think she was always happy and sad during these years," Mr. Grumman confessed. "I hadn't noticed so much before, but that's a good description of her."

"You talk about her like it's in the past tense," Jordan observed.

Mr. Grumman sighed noticeably and said, "I don't think that girl exists anymore than that young man exists."

Mr. Grumman pointed at the picture of himself.

"But you're here," Jordan observed. "I've talked to the old woman—she does exist, doesn't she? My brother's friends never notice her and think I'm crazy sometimes."

"You're not crazy," Mr. Grumman smiled. "Lydie does still exist, but like me she's changed through the years. I was almost twenty in the photograph—Lydie, a few years younger. I thought I could do and accomplish anything and everything but then—but then life gets in the way. It wears you down somehow to where you almost forget the things that used to be important."

"I don't understand," Jordan confessed.

Mr. Grumman laughed, which surprised Jordan. She could scarcely think Mr. Grumman would ever have a happy thought to cause him to laugh.

"I don't imagine you can," Mr. Grumman smiled. "You're just a girl. You have your whole life ahead of you. You can literally make that life anything you want. I've had my time. I'm the sum of all my decisions and have more life behind me than in front of me. Life is about consequences and rewards and I have to live with my choices."

"Don't you still have choices?" Jordan asked. "It seems to me adults get to make all the choices. Where we live, what we do."

Mr. Grumman thought for a moment before saying, "You're pretty wise for a young girl. I guess we do all have choices."

Mr. Grumman looked as if he would say more before sighing deeply.

"It's almost five," he finally said. "You'd better get home."

Jordan nodded and headed to the front room.

"Your mother was right," Mr. Grumman said, as Jordan stepped to the porch. "You are a good worker. If you'll come back on Friday, I'll have some more chores for you."

"The stones in back," Jordan timidly inquired. "What are they?"

Mr. Grumman looked perturbed at the question. "I guess they're pretty silly to have in a backyard. They're my stones. I used to carve and later made a living by carving the names of people in their gravestone. A gravestone is a powerful piece of rock. It tells the date a person is born and the date they pass from this life. The hyphen in between is all that's left to remember them."

"But why do you have them in your yard," Jordan asked. "They're not—"

"Buried back there," Mr. Grumman interrupted. "No. They're stones that were damaged or had to be replaced. I imagined I might try my hand at sculpture someday, but mostly the stones just sit there waiting."

Mr. Grumman looked at the young girl on his porch and said, "I'll see you Friday?"

Jordan nodded, as Mr. Grumman handed her a ten dollar bill. She walked away and could hear the door to Mr. Grumman's house shut behind her. As much as she had wanted to get out of the house, the sound saddened her. She thought of Mr. Grumman spending his days alone in the house and she felt sorry for him. Jordan was also puzzled about Mr. Grumman's talk about choices. She wondered what choices he had made in his past to make him seem so sad.

CHAPTER 24

An empty yard greeted Jordan as she approached her house. Although only a few minutes after five o'clock, the winter sky already draped a steely gray over the darkening horizon as evening approached. Jordan watched television a few minutes, but was restless after working for Mr. Grumman.

"I'll bake a cake," Jordan whispered to herself.

She smiled mightily at the idea of doing something constructive. Jordan rummaged through the kitchen and quickly mixed two cups of flour with two cups of sugar. Carefully reading the recipe, she added cocoa, baking soda, three eggs, baking powder, salt, and oil. Jordan returned to the refrigerator for the last ingredient, milk. A panicked Jordan searched for the carton of milk before letting out a muffled scream. The milk was gone.

"It's okay," Jordan calmly whispered to herself. "I've got ten dollars and the Safeway store is a block away."

Jordan quickly pulled on her coat and stepped into the cool evening. The wind whipped through the leafless trees. The overcast sky made the evening look even later than it was. Jordan walked around the corner and for the first time in her life, she did not feel nervous about walking past Mr. Grumman's house. Fourteenth Street was busy this time of the evening, but Jordan had no problems crossing the road and soon she was under the shelter of the store's awning. As Jordan stepped toward the door, the glass doors swung open automatically. A sign reading, "No Shirt, No Shoes, No Service" hung over another sign saying, "No pets allowed."

Thunder rumbled faintly in the distance, causing Jordan to study the ominous sky. With rain threatening, Jordan hurried inside. She had been to the store countless times and moved quickly to the milk counter in the back of the store. Jordan hesitated for a moment, deciding whether to buy a pint or a quart of milk. As she walked by the refrigerated shelves, Jordan felt something warm and soft brush against her ankle. A sable colored cat wandering the aisles startled her.

Recognizing the cat immediately, Jordan said, "What are you doing here?"

The cat stared at her with a cool indifference.

Jordan knelt down to pet the cat when she heard, "There you are!"

Jordan looked up to see the cat's owner ambling toward her. Jordan picked up the cat and waited for Lydie to approach.

"Are you trying to get lost?" the old woman scolded as she talked plainly to the cat.

"I just found her," Jordan explained.

"She's not even supposed to be in here," Lydie whispered. "I had her in the cart and the next thing I know she's gone."

"Here," Jordan said as she handed the old woman the cat.

The woman gingerly took the cat and placed her in the cart, as she looked around to see if she had attracted any undue attention.

"I haven't seen you wandering around in a few days," the old woman noted.

"No ma'am," Jordan responded. "I've been working."

"It's good for a young woman to learn a vocation," the woman replied.

"I'm cleaning house for Mr. Grumman," Jordan continued.

"Teddy?" the old woman asked with a heightened interest.

Jordan nodded awkwardly before saying cheerfully, "I saw a photograph of you today."

"What!" the concerned woman exclaimed. "What kind of picture would Teddy have of me?"

Jordan looked down at her shoes nervously before saying, "It was a picture of a play. I think you were Juliet."

"Oh," the woman said in a relieved tone. "That was a long time ago."

"Mr. Grumman said it was before 1920," Jordan explained.

"Yes, a very long time ago," the woman repeated. "Well, I'd better finish shopping before the store owner catches me with this cat."

Without further conversation the woman wheeled her cart away from Jordan and down an aisle. Jordan could not help but watch the old woman as she slowly ambled away. Jordan sensed the woman wanted to go unnoticed, but she wore the same odd, strangely old clothes, which made her conspicuous in the busy store. Lydie held a matted blanket of some kind, with which she attempted to hide the cat. Jordan noticed the customers in front of the old woman avoided eye contact and ignored the strange character. However, the people out of the woman's sight were obviously studying her and even whispering about the odd woman's appearance in the store. Jordan watched the people for a moment and realized they were not mocking the woman, but were looking at her as if she were some type of celebrity.

Jordan heard another ominous rumbling of thunder and quickly grabbed a pint of milk and headed to the checkout stand. After paying for her milk, Jordan stepped outside to a deluge of rain pouring from the now dark sky.

"You should wear a raincoat like me," Lydie said as she stood outside the store watching the rain.

"I guess," a discouraged Jordan replied, watching the rain puddle in the parking lot in front of her.

Jordan's house was only a block away, but she would be soaked in the cold rain if she tried to run for it. Looking at the sky, Jordan frowned and thought she would be getting wet and cold.

"Mrs. Marland," a voice from behind greeted the old woman standing by Jordan.

Lydie turned around suspiciously, as if perturbed at the interruption and said, "Yes."

"It's Marsha Keathly," the woman replied. "I live a few blocks from you."

"Oh yes," Lydie said. "I didn't recognize you."

"Do you need a ride?" Marsha asked. "I'm heading home now and it won't be out of the way."

"That would be fine," a hesitant Lydie replied. "If it's not out of your way?"

"Not at all," the enthusiastic Marsha said. "I'll pull the car up after they've loaded my groceries."

Lydie watched the heavy rain and then looked at the girl standing close to her under the awning. "I need to get this girl home, as well. Will that be a problem?"

The surprised woman who had offered the ride hesitated a second before Lydie added, "She lives right around the corner."

"That won't be any problem at all," the woman assured her.

The woman left to get her car before Lydie said to Jordan, "I hope you don't mind a lift in this rain."

"No," Jordan replied. "How did you know I lived around the corner?"

Lydie looked at Jordan and factually stated, "You told me the first time we met. Besides that, when you said you were cleaning house for Teddy Grumman, I could only assume you were neighbors."

Jordan stared at the old woman, admiring her deductive ability.

"I'm not crazy," Lydie added. "I'm just old. Things aren't always what they seem with people. I know everyone in this town has their eyes on me. They don't have me fooled. Sometimes you just need a ride home."

Jordan did not respond and the old woman stood silently at the curb after her speech. In a few moments Marsha Keathly pulled a dark-colored sedan to the front of the store. The car looked black in the dark rain, but Jordan could see it was a burgundy color. The driver helped Lydie into the front seat and motioned Jordan into the backseat. The car had lush velvet seats and still had that new car smell as Jordan watched the raindrops beading on the window.

"Is this a Cadillac?" Lydie asked as the woman began to drive away.

Lydie gently rubbed a "C" adorning the front dash.

"It's a Caprice," Marsha explained. "It's made by Chevrolet."

"Very nice," Lydie replied. "I always liked Cadillac's ride. Mr. Marland was a Cadillac man."

"This is like the Cadillac for Chevrolet," the driver nervously said, obviously trying to make polite conversation.

"It's very nice," Lydie assured her as she cradled the cat in her lap.

"Where does your friend live?" Marsha asked.

"Tell her, Jordan," Lydie commanded.

Jordan was surprised the old woman remembered her name, but said, "If you'll turn the corner on to 13th Street, it's the third house from the corner."

In less than a minute, the car pulled in front of the Bennett's house and Jordan opened the door to get out.

"Thank you for the ride," Jordan said to the driver, who watched her in the mirror.

"You're welcome," the driver replied.

"I'll be seeing you," Lydie said with an expressionless face. "Tell Teddy Grumman to keep his memories to himself."

Wondering what Lydie had meant by her strange farewell, Jordan stepped out of the car and walked hurriedly to the safety of the small front porch of her house.

CHAPTER 25

"Do you know anything about the old woman that lives next to the Marland Mansion?" Jordan asked when she saw Linda Pelletier the next day at school.

"Huh?" a puzzled Linda replied.

"The woman that lives next to the Marland Mansion," Jordan explained. "I think she used to be a Marland. Her name is Lydie."

"Don't know her," Linda confessed. "Why do you ask?"

"No reason," Jordan claimed.

Jordan's curiosity about the old woman had grown since seeing the picture of a younger Lydie in the photograph at Mr. Grumman's house.

"You got your theme paper done?" Linda asked.

"No," Jordan frowned.

"Have you started?" Linda quizzed with a raised eyebrow.

"Some," Jordan replied. "I've got a topic and read a little about her in the school library."

"What's the topic?" Linda inquired.

"I'm doing my report on Anastasia," Jordan confided cautiously.

"That'll be cool," Linda replied. "I actually thought about her myself. Great minds think alike."

"Maybe," Jordan smiled. "I thought she was interesting."

"Not interesting, intriguing," Linda grinned. "The lost daughter of the Czar...that'd be pretty cool to learn you were royalty."

Jordan frowned and replied, "I don't really know much more than I've read in the *World Book*. I've got to get on it this weekend."

"Me too," Linda shrugged. "Why don't we head to the library Saturday?"

"I need to go," Jordan confessed. "What time?"

"I'll pick you up about nine," Linda smiled, showing her shiny braces.

Jordan did some more research in the small school library about Anastasia and felt more confident about her topic choice. She was getting a better idea of the types of information she needed for the report and was looking forward to spending Saturday with Linda. Mrs. Pelletier arrived at the Bennett house a little before nine o'clock the next morning to take the girls to the city's library.

"Hello, Mrs. Pelletier," Jordan said timidly as she settled into the backseat.

"Hello, Jordan," Mrs. Pelletier replied.

After a brief pause, Mrs. Pelletier said, "You're not going to run off on me, are you?"

Jordan fidgeted nervously and replied, "No. I think I learned my lesson about getting lost."

Mrs. Pelletier smiled pleasantly, as she looked at Jordan through the rearview mirror.

"Maybe my mom can answer your question," Linda interrupted. "She's lived here forever."

"What question?" Jordan asked.

"The question about the old woman that lives by the mansion," Linda explained.

"Oh," Jordan muttered.

"What old woman?" Mrs. Pelletier asked.

Jordan hesitated briefly before saying, "There's a woman who lives in a house by the big mansion. I think her name is—"

"Lydie," Mrs. Pelletier interrupted. "Lydie Marland."

"Yes," Jordan replied. "That's her."

"Why are you interested in Mrs. Marland?" Mrs. Pelletier asked.

"I've met her a couple of times and was curious about her," Jordan explained.

"You've met Lydie Marland?" a surprised Mrs. Pelletier asked while looking at Jordan through the rearview mirror.

"I've talked to her a few times," Jordan admitted.

"Wow," Mrs. Pelletier sighed. "That's news."

"Why?" Linda asked.

"She's very reclusive," Mrs. Pelletier explained. "She's Ponca City's mystery woman for sure."

"Why is she so mysterious?" Jordan asked.

"Probably because she wants to be," Mrs. Pelletier reasoned. "She stays to herself and avoids most people. My friend, Erma Chamberlin, tried to interview her for a class she was taking on Oklahoma history and Lydie Marland flat out refused to talk about anything."

Jordan had more questions, but Mrs. Pelletier had already pulled in front of the library. She dropped the girls off in front of the building with strict instructions for Linda to be out front at noon. Linda waved as her mother drove away and the two girls faced the large, buff-bricked building housing the Ponca City Library. Jordan noticed the entrance featured three arches that reminded her of the opening to the boathouse at the Marland Mansion.

The girls separated. Linda looked up articles about Greta Garbo in the periodical index; while Jordan headed to the card catalogue to find books the library might have about Anastasia. Jordan found her topic interesting, but hard to research. Facts about the Grand Princess were few, but theories about her disappearance were many. Jordan learned Anastasia was the youngest of four royal daughters and that the family was disappointed that she was not a male heir. She had been born in 1901 and her family had been captured and executed when she was only 17 years old. Most thought Anastasia perished with her family, but some believed she had escaped and was in hiding from those who wished to do her harm.

The communists executed the Romanov family, but the grave of Anastasia had never been found. Jordon studied several pictures of the young woman showing a round-faced young girl who had blossomed into an attractive young woman. She had a mischievous shape to her mouth, which caused Jordan to believe the woman held some deep secret. Jordan found a book about Anastasia and a woman named Anna Anderson who claimed to be the lost princess. After an hour, Jordan had a good idea how she would write her report. She carefully copied a few pages from magazine articles on the photocopier and checked out a book to take home.

Jordan's interest in Anastasia began when she watched a television show about the Grand Princess called *Anastasia: The Mystery of Anna.* The television mini-series caught her attention and she was sure she could come up with five pages based on the information she found in the library. As interested as Jordan had become in the story of the lost princess, another mystery was starting to fascinate her. Jordan looked around the library to see that Linda was still copying articles for her report. She headed to the card catalogue and looked up Marland, but did not find much. Jordan then looked in the periodic index to find several articles about the Marlands and Ponca City.

As Jordan sat at the plain library table and scanned the titles, she began thinking about the old woman she knew so little about. Something had bothered Jordan about Lydie's story, but she could not get things clear in her mind until she was sitting in the quietness of the library. Lydie had told her about coming to Ponca City as a girl and living with her rich aunt and uncle. She had explained to Jordan that she had been adopted by the Marlands and described the elaborate parties and the luxurious mansion that had been her home.

Lydie never married, Jordan thought to herself.

The old woman herself had told Jordan she was Lydie Marland and that she had taken the last name of her adoptive parents. Mrs. Pelletier however had called her Mrs. Marland. Marsha Keathly, the woman who had given Jordan a ride home, had also called the old woman Mrs. Marland. Jordan believed she had misheard the title, but as she thought back, she was confident the women used Mrs. instead of Miss when talking about Lydie. If Lydie was a Mrs., her name would certainly not be Marland, Jordan reasoned.

Jordan quickly looked at the list of periodicals to find some explanation. There did not seem to be anything until she saw an article in the November 22, 1958 edition of the *Saturday Evening Post*.

The provocative title read, *Where is Lyde Marland?*

Jordan whispered the description to the story as she read, "This governor's widow was last seen on a Midwestern highway in 1953. Is she alive? Is she in hiding? Here are the strange facts."

Jordan moved to the rack of periodicals and quickly located *The Saturday Evening Post* section. She felt like a detective about to break the big case as she eased the shelf up to reveal the boxes of back issues stored there.

Will the library have periodicals going back so far? Jordan thought to herself.

Jordon quickly looked at the label at the end of each box. She found some 1960s boxes. Her heart raced when she spotted "1958" neatly stenciled on the front of one of the boxes. Jordan pulled the dusty box to inspect the contents and thumbed through the magazines looking for the November 22 issue. Jordan's heart sank as she located November 15 and November 29. Her issue was missing. Jordan frantically searched again in case the magazine was out of place.

Jordan was about to ask the librarian for help when Linda whispered, "It's noon. Are you ready to go?"

Jordan remembered Mrs. Pelletier's admonishment to Linda to be out front at noon. Jordan decided she had better not test Linda's mother again so she nodded. The girls gathered their notes and walked into a cool but sunny day. Mrs. Pelletier was waiting and seemed relieved to see the girls on time. Jordan took a look back at the library, determined to learn more about the Lydie Marland mystery.

CHAPTER 26

"How was it?" Mrs. Pelletier asked as she drove away from the library.

"It was the library, Mom," Linda sighed. "Old books and a lot of quiet."

"Oh," Mrs. Pelletier frowned. "Did you finish?"

"Not quite," Linda said, "but I've got all my notes and should be finished by Monday."

"How about you, Jordan?" Mrs. Pelletier asked.

"I found some good articles and a book on Anastasia," Jordan replied. "I won't be finished Monday, but I'll be close."

"Would you girls like some lunch?" Mrs. Pelletier asked.

Linda looked at Jordan to get an approving look before saying pleasantly, "Sure."

"Mikey D's?" Mrs. Pelletier asked.

"Sure," Linda replied, trying not to smirk at her mother's attempt to talk like a kid.

At lunch, Jordan worked up the nerve to ask, "Mrs. Pelletier, when you were talking about the old woman that lives by the mansion, you called her Mrs. Marland. How is that possible? She told me she was the adopted daughter. If she married, wouldn't she have a different last name?"

Mrs. Pelletier almost choked on her drink.

The nervous woman looked around the restaurant to insure they were sitting away from other customers before saying, "You haven't heard the story?"

Jordan shook her head, while Linda apathetically listened while munching on some fries.

Mrs. Pelletier leaned toward Jordan and said in a soft voice, "Lydie was adopted by Mr. and Mrs. Marland. She was Mrs. Marland's niece, I believe."

"That's what she told me," Jordan confirmed. "She said they had great parties and lived in the big house on Grand Street until they moved to the big mansion on the hill."

"They didn't all make it to the new mansion," Mrs. Pelletier coyly replied. "The first Mrs. Marland got sick and died before the house was completed. That didn't slow Mr. Marland down much. He still had his grand parties and busied himself with building his company. His company turned into Conoco south of town. Lydie ran things at the house. Eventually, Mr. Marland had the adoption annulled and Lydie became the second Mrs. Marland."

"What!" a suddenly energized Linda exclaimed. "He married his daughter!"

"Keep your voice down," Mrs. Pelletier admonished Linda, as she scanned the restaurant to make sure they had not attracted unwanted attention.

"That's gross," Linda stated in a softer tone.

"She wasn't his real daughter," Mrs. Pelletier pointed out. "She was his wife's niece."

"Still," Linda said. "He was old enough to be her father."

"I suppose it was a marriage of convenience," Mrs. Pelletier stated. "Someone needed to tend to the social affairs and Lydie fit that bill."

"That must have been quite a scandal," Jordan commented. "Maybe that's why she keeps away from people."

"She wasn't always so shy," Mrs. Pelletier shared. "Mr. Marland became a congressman and later the tenth governor of Oklahoma. She was first lady, after all."

"Our governor was married to his own daughter!" Linda smirked.

"Keep your voice down," Mrs. Pelletier warned again. "It was a different time. Mr. Marland died and Mrs. Marland has been—eccentric since then."

"When was that?" a curious Jordan asked.

"I'm not really sure," Mrs. Pelletier answered. "It was before I was born."

"Wow, before the Civil War," Linda teased her mother.

"Not quite," Mrs. Pelletier smiled. "But all that happened years ago."

The conversation drifted away from Lydie Marland, but Jordan could not quit thinking about the strange old woman who had befriended her. When Jordan returned home, she tried to concentrate on the report on Anastasia. She managed to scribble out a rough draft, but her interest was focused on the intriguing past of the strange woman living less than a mile from her front door.

CHAPTER 27

Jordan finished her paper on Anastasia, although her interests in Lydie Marland had been a distraction. The next Tuesday after school, Jordan trudged down the street to clean house for Mr. Grumman. She had gotten over her fear of going to his house, but she would rather have stayed home during her afternoons. Mr. Grumman greeted Jordan coolly. He did try to smile, however, and he seemed more comfortable about her being in his house.

Jordan began her work in the kitchen and continued her routine through the house. By the time she was ready to vacuum, Mr. Grumman had dozed off in his chair in the front room. She needed to sweep, but decided to not disturb her employer. She took the opportunity to explore Mr. Grumman's "memories" room instead.

The door squeaked slightly, but Mr. Grumman continued his napping. Jordan quickly moved to the stack of photographs where she had seen Lydie Marland's picture on her previous visit to the room. Jordan did not see any pictures of Lydie, but there were some photographs of Mr. Grumman's family. As Jordan looked around the room, there was something else that attracted her attention. In the corner, a stack of old magazines sat on the floor. Jordon could see a *Life* magazine and a *Look* magazine. The magazines were from the 1960s. As Jordan thumbed through the periodicals, her heart raced as she saw a copy of a *Saturday Evening Post*.

The cover showed a hand drawn image of a young wife supervising a man hanging wallpaper while her husband watched. The cover art did not interest Jordan, but the headline that read *Where Is Lyde Marland?* did. Jordan had seen the article referenced in the library, but could not locate the copy there. Jordan carefully picked up the old magazine and quickly found the article. For the next twenty minutes, she read a fascinating and bizarre tale.

The magazine from November of 1958 showed a large photograph of Lydie Marland in her early forties. Jordan would have had a hard time recognizing the picture as the old woman she had interacted with the past months, but the photograph looked strikingly similar to the painting of the younger Lydie she had seen in the mansion. The photograph showed an attractive woman with an air of resignation. Her short brown hair and delicate features were mismatched with her sad eyes that seemed to focus on some unseen past.

The magazine mentioned the poverty of Lydie's real parents and the extravagant life she led as the adopted daughter of a multi-millionaire. It described lavish parties, swimming pools, polo teams, and fox hunts—all the things Lydie herself had mentioned to Jordon. The article described the multi-million dollar mansion, which the Marlands lived in for less than two years. The fall of Mr. Marland's oil empire and the decline in his personal fortune were discussed. In the end, his new bride was left with little and lived in the modest house next to the great mansion.

According to the article, Mr. Marland was 54 when he married his 26 year old adopted daughter in the mid 1920s. Mr. Marland later became a United States Congressman before becoming the tenth governor of Oklahoma. The article claimed Lydie had been involved in a failed romance after the death of Mr. Marland and that she had unresolved issues with her family. She vanished in 1953 and as of 1958 was a missing person.

"You're in here again," Mr. Grumman barked from the doorway.

Jordan tried to hide the magazine, but it was a large publication and Mr. Grumman could not help but see it in her hand.

"I wouldn't let Lydie Marland know you're reading that," Mr. Grumman commented.

Jordan put the magazine back in its stack and asked, "Why?"

"She would think you're spying on her," Mr. Grumman explained.

"Why do you have this?" Jordan asked referring to the old magazine.

"I told you," he answered, "this is my memories room. I collect all kinds of things. It's not often someone you know is the subject of a *Saturday Evening Post* article."

"It said she disappeared," Jordan stated.

"As far as anyone around here knew, she vanished," Mr. Grumman replied. "Lydie left one day and no one saw her again for twenty-two years."

"Why?" Jordan asked.

Mr. Grumman picked up the old magazine and said, "I don't think anyone really knows—that is besides Lydie. I'm not sure she even knows for sure. I wouldn't put too much stock in this article, however."

"Why not?" Jordan responded.

"This story has more speculation than actual facts," Mr. Grumman claimed. "I've lived in town long enough to have heard all of the rumors relating to the Marlands and particularly Lydie. I think the truth of Lydie's life is probably more tragic than mysterious."

"The whole thing is made up?" Jordan clarified.

"I didn't say that," Mr. Grumman corrected. "I said you have to be careful about information that comes from somebody's opinion. Confusing opinion with truth is always a dangerous activity."

"Lydie loved her husband very much and felt lost when he died," Mr. Grumman continued. "Lydie had not been trained or encouraged to learn any occupation. I think Lydie left town because she wanted to be left alone."

"Like Greta Garbo," Jordan whispered.

Mr. Grumman looked at the young girl and said, "What do you know about Greta Garbo?"

"Not much," Jordan confessed. "My friend did a paper on her and said she retired in the prime of her career and wanted to be left alone."

Mr. Grumman chuckled to himself and said, "That's a good analogy. I used to watch Greta Garbo at the movies in town when I was a kid. Lydie had a bit harder time than Greta Garbo at hiding out. The actress chose to hide from publicity, but I think Lydie felt she had to run from it. She lived off of what property she could salvage from the estate, but life must have been difficult for her. It's hard to live without, but it would be harder when you're accustomed to having so much."

"Why does the article spell her name Lyde?" Jordan asked.

"Lydie always spelled her name L Y D I E as far as I know," Mr. Grumman said. "It may be that her real name was L Y D E or it could be the name was spelled phonetically for some reason."

"What do you think happened to her during those years?" Jordan inquired.

Mr. Grumman shrugged his shoulders and answered, "I think she was hiding. I think she did what she could to survive and that it's her business. Most people in town respect that. If you want to keep in her good graces, I would suggest you do the same."

Jordan nodded and said, "I need to sweep and then I'll be finished."

Mr. Grumman looked around the small room and said, "How much dust can an old man create in one week? Why don't you vacuum next time and call it a day?"

"Yes, sir," Jordan smiled.

Mr. Grumman paid Jordan her ten dollars and she walked out into the remnant of the winter's afternoon. She had some of the questions answered about Lydie Marland, but Jordan would learn that Mr. Grumman had secrets of his own.

CHAPTER 28

Saturday was a relatively warm day for late January. A few mounds of gray snow drifts remained in the shady areas from a storm a few days earlier, but calm winds and brilliant sunny skies made for a nice winter day. Jordan needed to go to the library and had delayed asking her mother, hoping she could go with Linda. Her friend, however, had been sick and missed school the last couple of days. The library was within walking distance, so Jordan decided to walk there a little before noon.

Jordan walked by Mr. Grumman's silent and lonely house. She did not have the sense of dread she had before. Jordan actually liked her part-time job cleaning his house. Her visits with the old man also proved interesting. He loved the town's history and seemed to enjoy sharing his thoughts with her. Jordan walked two blocks down 13th Street to Grand Avenue, which was the main street into downtown. Jordan stayed on the north side of the street and soaked up the warm sun. To the south, white streams of steam from the refinery lazily drifted into the azure blue sky. Two blocks to the west, Jordan admired a large white house with a red tile roof. This house had been the first Marland home. Jordan tried to imagine what the parties might have been like in the eight acre garden that was now home for a neighborhood of nice brick houses.

For the first time in a while, Jordan felt some peace inside her. It had been a difficult time for her family, but the warm winter's day with a hint of spring in the air made her imagine a better future. Her good mood increased when she saw J.J. Reynolds sweeping a porch on one of the large houses bordering the old Marland home.

The normally reserved Jordan carefully crossed the street and walked quickly toward her brother's friend. J.J. toiled apathetically and she smiled at the lazy way he carried himself as he maneuvered the broom around curved steps leading up to an impressive home.

"Never thought I'd see you sweeping," Jordan cheerfully teased, as she walked up behind the young man.

J.J. Reynolds turned around and said, "Hey, Jordan."

Jordan blushed slightly when the handsome boy called her "Jordan" instead of his normally exaggerated "JorDAN."

"Making some extra money?" she asked.

J.J. looked around nervously, as if embarrassed that someone would see him, and replied, "Kinda, I guess."

Jordan's good mood evaporated in an instant when she looked in the driveway and noticed the pickup truck belonging to the man who had demanded the rent from her mother. Jordan was deflated to think J.J. worked for the landlord who had embarrassed her weeks before.

Before Jordan could ask about J.J.'s employer, the front door opened and Jordan was horrified to see the rent collector standing there.

The man stared at Jordan in a way that left no doubt she was not welcome.

Looking past the young girl, the man barked, "You better have this porch sparkle, Jerome."

J.J. nodded, as the man said forcefully, "I'm not kidding, son."

The man gave Jordan one more disapproving look and disappeared inside the house.

Jordan stood speechless as J.J. continued to sweep.

"Your name is Jerome?" Jordan finally was able to ask.

J.J. nodded and added, "Jerome Jefferson to be exact, but only my family calls me Jerome so don't go tellin' anyone."

"You live here?" Jordan numbly asked.

J.J. again nodded.

"That's your dad," Jordan reasoned. "That's why you took off that day."

"Hey," J.J. reasoned. "A guy can't help what his father does. He owns a lot of real estate and manages property all over town. I didn't know he was coming to your house."

"You work for him?" Jordan asked.

"Not exactly," J.J. sighed. "I took his truck for little ride the other night and the cops pulled me over. This is my penitence. Dad had to pay my ticket and I've got to work it off doing nothing jobs like sweeping the porch that will be covered in leaves next time the wind blows."

"I've got to go," Jordan claimed.

"What are you doing down here anyway?" J.J. asked.

"I've got to go to the library," Jordan explained.

"Oh," J.J. smirked. "I'll see you around JorDAN."

Jordan walked away and J.J. Reynolds continued sweeping. Jordan always imagined J.J. lived on the wrong side of the tracks and might even understand some of the financial challenges the Bennetts had endured the past year. As Jordan turned back to look at J.J., she remembered what Mr. Grumman had said, "Things aren't always what they seem."

CHAPTER 29

Jordan walked away from J.J. Reynolds with a sickening feeling of uncertainty. The winter's sun hung brightly in the cloudless blue sky, but to Jordan the colors seemed muted and surreal. The library was only a few blocks away, and Jordan walked listlessly toward it. Mothers shepherding young children into the library somehow made Jordan feel even more alone.

Jordan's head slumped down as she walked lethargically, unaware of the Saturday traffic moving around her. As Jordan turned to enter the library, something caught her attention that snapped her out of her malaise. A block from the library, a frail, old woman shuffled down the sidewalk in an erratic stagger. Jordan immediately recognized the eccentric wardrobe of Lydie Marland.

School and a part-time job had prevented Jordan from walking to the Marland Mansion for several weeks. Jordan had wanted to visit the old woman and ask some questions about her curious past. Jordan walked quickly and overtook the woman who seemed to be walking aimlessly.

"Mrs. Marland," Jordan greeted her.

For a moment, Jordan thought the old woman would try to walk away, but then she turned around and looked cautiously at the approaching girl.

"Are you okay?" a concerned Jordan asked.

"Of course," Lydie quickly replied. "Why would you ask such a question?"

"You're a long ways from home," Jordan explained. "I was wondering how you were going to get back."

"I have a taxi coming," Lydie assured her.

The old woman studied Jordan for a second and asked, "What are you doing downtown?"

"I'm going to the library to return a book," Jordan replied.

Lydie nodded positively at the answer and said, "Let me see."

Jordan handed Lydie her book and the woman carefully examined the front cover. The old woman slowly moved the book closer until she held it only a few inches from her eyes.

"You'll have to help me," the old woman finally sighed. "What is the book about?"

"Anastasia," Jordan answered.

"Anastasia?" Lydie replied.

Jordan nodded as the woman continued to stare at the book's cover, although it was apparent she could not see it well.

"What's your interest in the Grand Duchess?" Lydie inquired.

"I wrote a theme paper for English on her," Jordan explained.

"Interesting," Lydie observed. "And what did you learn?"

"Her family was taken prisoner," Jordan began. "It was when the communists took over Russia. After a time, her family was shot."

"And Anastasia?" Lydie asked.

"No one really knows," Jordan replied. "They never found her body and—a lot of people think she escaped."

"Not very likely," Lydie sighed.

"It was a long time ago," Jordan confessed. "I guess she would be gone by now anyway."

The response caused Lydie to look carefully at the young girl before she asked in an almost playful tone, "You've done research on the Grand Duchess?"

Jordan nodded.

"When was she born?" Lydie questioned.

Jordan had spent days reading and learning about the enigmatic girl and replied, "June 18, 1901."

Lydie tried to hide a smirking smile as she asked, "And how old would she be?"

Jordan quickly calculated in her head and said, "Eighty-five?"

"Oh my, that would be old," Lydie said. "I guess it would surprise you to learn that I'm a full year older than the Grand Duchess?"

Jordan did not know how to respond, but she finally muttered, "Really?"

The old woman had a sudden energy to her as she nodded.

Jordan asked, "So she could still be alive?"

"I wouldn't think so," Lydie replied. "What do you think?"

"She could have escaped, I guess," Jordan reasoned. "She wouldn't be that old. This book says a woman claimed to be her, but I don't know."

"That's always a good answer," the old woman said with a tilt to her head. "I don't know."

"What do you think?" Jordan asked.

Lydie answered in a solemn and serious tone, "I think she died with her family—alone and unglamorously. The rest is silly romance. People always like to speculate about things they see as mysteries, but the truth is usually stark and bleak and uninteresting."

"But she could've escaped?" Jordan interjected.

Lydie thought for a moment and said, "Possibly. I think if she did escape she would have been content to stay away. The notoriety of royalty and wealth got her entire family executed. Why would a person want that life? I would have stayed away from the prying eyes and the people bent on using any semblance of fame."

"I would have revealed myself," Jordan replied. "Who wouldn't want to be a princess?"

"Anyone who's ever been a princess," the old woman stated flatly. "All young girls dream of being some secret royalty—entitled to be pampered and treated as if being of some importance, but it all leads to misery and disillusionment. Be happy with what you've got—even if you think it's not much. You'll find life's not so much getting what you want but learning to want what you have. If Anastasia survived, she'd have been better off being a pauper than a princess. Better not to know what you've sacrificed."

The old woman spoke as if giving a speech to an audience that was not there. Jordan had wanted to ask the woman a question for many weeks. She had learned some things about Lydie Marland and knew of her twenty-two year disappearance from Ponca City. Jordan wanted to know why she had left and what she had done for those missing years. No one in town, including Mr. Grumman, seemed willing to answer those questions. Jordan could never determine if people did not know or did not like to talk about those times.

"I was wondering—" Jordan tentatively began.

Lydie looked at the young girl as if bracing for a question about which she did not want to think.

"My ride's here," Lydie said, interrupting Jordan's question.

The old woman handed the book back to Jordan and quickly gathered her things. She was a whirl of activity and in a moment a city taxi pulled up and a man quickly jumped out of the car to help Mrs. Marland into the backseat. Lydie avoided eye contact and did not give the girl an opening to ask any questions. The car door slammed and Lydie Marland looked out the closed window at the perplexed young girl. As the taxi drove away, Jordan could see fright and foreboding in the old woman's eyes. Jordan's curiosity was overwhelmed by feelings of sympathy for her. Answers would have to come at another time, and Jordan believed they would have to come from someone besides Lydie Marland.

CHAPTER 30

Jordan earned an "A" for her paper on Anastasia. She wanted to celebrate with Linda, but her new friend had been absent all week. Jordan had become accustomed to eating lunch each day with Linda. She enjoyed the girl's clever observations and pleasant disposition. The lunch hour became lonely and long without her friend.

When the bell rang at 3:15 on Friday afternoon, Jordan breathed a sigh of relief. She wanted to start her weekend, but instead, Jordan boarded the bus heading north. Jordan took a seat in the middle of the bus and tried to avoid eye contact with students she barely knew.

The bus made three stops before coming to Linda Pelletier's neighborhood. Jordan scampered out of the bus with four other kids. The bus driver looked oddly at her when he realized he had an extra passenger, but Jordan ducked her head and walked toward Linda's house.

The Pelletier's neighborhood featured a street neatly lined with new brick homes and well trimmed yards. Linda's house was a single story, buff-brick home with the Pelletier's Jeep parked in front. Jordan had been to the house a couple of times and always fought a nagging feeling of jealousy when she saw it. She did not think it was fair for the Pelletiers to have the large home, the great car, and the perfect family. Jordan did not begrudge Linda her prosperity, but wished she had some of her friend's good fortune.

Jordan rang the doorbell hoping Linda would answer, but reasoned that her friend must be sick, since she had been absent from school the past week. In a few seconds, Jordan could hear muffled noises coming from inside as Mrs. Pelletier opened the door.

"Jordan?" Mrs. Pelletier greeted her. "What are you doing here?"

"I came to see Linda," Jordan meekly explained.

Mrs. Pelletier looked different to Jordan. Her normally groomed hair was somewhat matted and messy. Her eyes were puffy and red. Jordan could tell she had been crying.

"That's nice," Mrs. Pelletier said. "You should have called—Linda's been—sick."

"I figured," Jordan nervously replied.

Jordan knew she should have called before coming over, but the phone in the Bennett house had been disconnected for several weeks.

"How did you get here?" Mrs. Pelletier asked, as she looked at the empty street.

"I took the bus," Jordan explained.

"I'm sorry," Mrs. Pelletier said. "I'm being rude. Won't you come in?"

Jordan followed Mrs. Pelletier inside and noticed the house was not as immaculate as it had been in the past.

"Things have been a little out of sorts," Mrs. Pelletier explained, as she fought back tears. "I'll see if Linda's awake."

"Is Linda okay?" a concerned Jordan asked.

Mrs. Pelletier did not answer immediately and cried softly in front of Jordan before saying, "We're not sure. She's always been so sickly, but we've been in the hospital most of this week."

"Oh my," Jordan muttered.

Wiping her eyes, Mrs. Pelletier said as she walked away, "I'll check on Linda—wait here."

Jordan stood by the front door a few anxious minutes before Mrs. Pelletier motioned her to come to Linda's room. Jordan walked timidly past Mrs. Pelletier to see Linda lying in her bed. Linda looked pale and tired, but her braces-filled smile made Jordan feel immediately better.

"Hey," Linda smiled.

Jordan walked to a chair next to the bed and asked, "What's going on?"

Linda looked past Jordan and said to her mother, "It's okay, Mom. I'll call you if I need anything."

Mrs. Pelletier looked at her daughter for a moment before reluctantly leaving the girls alone.

"I'm so glad to see you," Linda smiled. "I don't know what's worse, feeling bad or having Mom looking over me twenty-four hours a day."

"What's wrong?" Jordan asked again.

"I found out I'm diabetic," Linda calmly explained. "I hadn't felt well in a long time—you know, always tired and stuff like that. Last weekend I got real sick. I thought it was the flu or something. I threw-up my body weight, I think, and spent all day Saturday hugging the porcelain throne."

Although very concerned, Jordan could not help but smile at Linda's frank assessment of her illness.

"Are you better?" Jordan asked.

Linda looked strangely at her and nodded, "Sure, I'm feeling better—a little weak still. The doctor said I got dehydrated."

Jordan looked at Linda and knew her friend was not telling her everything. Linda's serious explanation and a worried look in her eye betrayed her.

"I've learned some stuff this week," Linda continued. "I learned diabetes doesn't go away. I've got to test my blood several times a day and I'm taking shots at least twice a day."

"For how long?" Jordan asked.

"Forever," Linda shrugged. "It's how I've got to keep my insulin in balance from now on."

Jordan did not say anything, but Linda could see her concern.

"It's okay," Linda assured her. "I'm feeling better and the doctor says I'll be back to normal soon. I'm already getting used to the shots. I'll be back to school next week. I promise."

Jordan and Linda talked for a while longer, until Mrs. Pelletier suggested her daughter needed rest. Jordan said good bye and Linda assured her again that things would be fine. Mrs. Pelletier offered to drive Jordan home, but Jordan could tell she did not want to leave Linda alone. Jordan easily convinced Mrs. Pelletier that she could walk home with little inconvenience. Jordan's house was a little more than a mile away and there was plenty of daylight.

After Mrs. Pelletier closed the door behind Jordan, the girl looked at the immaculately landscaped house and the new car in the driveway. Jordan had always seen Mrs. Pelletier as a woman wanting desperately to live vicariously through her daughter. Mrs. Pelletier kept her daughter in fashionable clothes and made sure Linda had all the advantages she could give. Jordan thought Mrs. Pelletier was sometimes embarrassed at her daughter's lack of social success. Today, however, Jordan watched a woman frightened for her daughter's future, and Mrs. Pelletier's veneer of self-importance was lost in concern for a clouded future for her daughter.

Jordan walked away from the Pelletier house with a sense of gratitude at having Linda as a friend. Linda had made her year bearable and Jordan now knew she would have the opportunity to reciprocate the kindness. Jordan realized what should have been evident for several months—Linda Pelletier was the best friend she would ever have.

The Pelletier's house was just north of the Country Club. Jordan crossed one busy street before making her way through the woods and to the Marland Mansion. The mansion was a little more than halfway home and Jordan still had over an hour of daylight left in the lengthening spring day. Jordan intended to head straight home, but a group of boys close to the boathouse caught her attention.

Jordan knew her brother would likely not be with the group. Brett had become more serious and introverted the past months and spent most of his afternoons working at the TG&Y store. Jordan looked over the group and did not see J.J. Reynolds or Brad Cooper. She did see Gump, Munchkin, and Peanut with a couple of other boys she did not recognize. Jordan almost walked away, but the boys were boisterously yelling, which roused Jordan's curiosity.

As Jordan stepped closer, she saw the boys holding a large paint bucket and twirling around until they became dizzy. The boy spinning with the bucket would stagger and wobble while the others laughed heartily. Jordan smiled at their foolishness, until she heard a painfully sharp shriek as the boys scrambled after something.

"Stop that!" Jordan screamed as she sprinted toward the boys.

The boys stared at the charging girl, while the smallest boy they called Munchkin forced a screeching cat into the paint bucket.

"Let her go!" Jordan yelled as she came closer.

The boys watched in sheepish silence as an out-of-breath Jordan confronted them.

"It's only Jordan," a relieved Peanut sighed.

"Let that cat go!" Jordan demanded angerily.

"We're not hurting her," Gump claimed. "We're just playing."

The boys had been taking turns spinning the five-gallon paint bucket with the cat forced inside and then chasing the angry dizzy cat.

"It doesn't look fun for the cat!" Jordan scolded.

Munchkin did not challenge the young girl and released the frantic cat from the large bucket. Jordan stared coldly at the boys as the cat scampered away.

"See," Gump noted. "The cat's fine."

"I'd like to stuff you in a can and see you get dizzy," Jordan huffed.

Gump looked at the other boys and teased, "That might be fun."

Jordan was in no mood to swap insults with the boys and walked away.

"Wait a minute," Gump said, which caused Jordan to stop a few feet away. "Where's your brother been?"

Jordan looked nervously at the boys that had been her brother's friends. She knew Brett had been embarrassed at his family's inability to pay bills and the rent. Brad Cooper had come by to see Brett a few times, but Jordan could tell a difference in her brother.

"He's been working," Jordan replied.

Gump studied the girl for a minute and said, "Tell'em not to be a stranger. Spring football will be starting soon and the coach wants to see him out there."

"I'll tell him," Jordan said.

"Sorry about the cat," Gump continued. "We're just killing time and the old cat was pretty funny when we let her out."

Jordan nodded and walked away from the boys. In a few minutes the boys wandered north and were soon out of sight. Jordan was about to walk around the large house, when she heard something rushing toward her.

Bending down, Jordan said in a soft voice, "Did you get away from those old boys, kitty?"

The cat looked at her nervously before rubbing against her leg. Jordan took a step and the cat followed.

"You better get home," Jordan instructed. "I can't promise those boys won't come back for you."

The cat let out a low rumble in her throat and continued to follow. Jordan knelt and was surprised to see the cat come into her arms.

"Are you scared?" Jordan said to the cat. "I've got you now."

The cat seemed content in her arms and Jordan said, "We better get you home."

Jordan carried the cat toward the house where Lydie Marland lived. The house was several hundred yards from the big mansion, but still inside the gates of the property. The modest-sized, buff-brick house was surrounded by a red brick courtyard. Jordan knocked timidly on the imposing planked oak door with heavy wrought-iron hardware, as she cradled the cat in her arms. Jordan heard nothing and put the cat on the ground before knocking more aggressively.

The house seemed silent and Jordan cautiously peeked in a window to see a sparsely furnished yet cluttered front room with a mattress in the middle of the floor.

"Can I help you?" a voice asked from behind Jordan.

Jordan turned to see a woman in her mid-forties walking toward her from the house next door.

"No," a nervous Jordan replied. "I found Mrs. Marland's cat and was trying to return her."

The woman looked at the young girl for a moment until the cat came to rub against Jordan's leg.

"The cat," the woman sighed.

Jordan nodded.

"Mrs. Marland has gone away," the woman claimed.

"Gone away?" Jordan questioned.

"She's been gone a couple of days," the woman said. "The cat has been hanging around and I haven't known what to do with her. She won't let me near her."

"Do you know where Mrs. Marland is?" Jordan asked.

"Not exactly," the woman warily admitted. "She hadn't been feeling well and I fear she's in the hospital or in a rest home. Mrs. Marland's not always the most forthcoming about her activities."

"Oh," Jordan replied. "Do you know when she'll be back?"

"No," the woman replied. "I guess you can leave the cat and I'll try to keep some food out."

Jordan nodded and walked away. The neighbor watched her for a moment before returning to her home. Jordan turned around when she heard the cat's throaty purr to see that the neighbor had gone inside.

"Go on," Jordan coaxed, but the cat looked at her with sad, lonely eyes. "Those boys won't bother you."

The cat continued to rub against Jordan and she reached down to have the cat jump into her arms. Jordan looked for some help, but no one seemed to be around. Hesitantly, she cradled the cat and started for home.

"You stealing that cat?" Winkie Dink teased, as his bicycle skidded to a stop a few feet away from Jordan.

"No!" Jordan quickly defended herself. "I'm taking care of her for a few days."

"I was just joshing," the large boy said as he leaned against his handlebars. "What'cha up to?"

"I'm going home," Jordan explained.

"I can ride with you," Winkie offered.

"I don't have a bike," Jordan replied. "Besides, I have to hold this cat."

"I'll ride slow," Winkie said.

Jordan did not look forward to a manufactured conversation with the awkward boy, but she could not come up with any reason for him to leave. Jordan breathed a sigh of relief, when she saw her brother Brett, J.J. Reynolds, and Brad Cooper walking up from the woods. Behind her, the boys who had been tormenting the cat also walked quickly toward her. On seeing the group of boys, Winkie Dink struggled to pedal his bicycle away.

"Wait a minute!" J.J. Reynolds shouted as he sprinted toward the chubby boy.

"Where you going Winkie Dink?" J.J. asked as he grabbed the boy's handlebars and prevented him from riding away.

"Nowhere," the boy replied.

"You're going nowhere in a hurry," J.J. sneered.

Gump, Peanut, and Munchkin had joined J.J. to block the boy's way while Brett and Brad Cooper were still approaching.

"I was just leaving," Winkie Dink said.

"Looked like you were bothering B.B.'s sister," J.J. teased. "I don't think B.B. would like to have a fat lard like you trying to sweet talk his little sis."

"He wasn't bothering me," Jordan said

"I didn't mean nothing," Winkie Dink pleaded.

J.J. Reynolds repeated the boy's answers in a mocking tone, "I didn't mean nothing. I didn't mean nothing."

Gump, Peanut, and Munchkin laughed, while the blushing Winkie Dink seemed to hunker down at their teasing. Brett and Brad Cooper were still walking toward the group, but seemed to be involved in their own conversation.

"You're a weirdo," J.J. continued. "A genuine pencil-necked geek with a ton of fat around that neck."

Winkie Dink did not respond as the boys continued to laugh.

"Don't tell me you're going to cry," J.J. taunted. "I don't think I can stand to see a blubbering toad lose it here in front of everyone."

Jordan had been annoyed by Winkie Dink's attention, but she now felt sorry for the large boy who fought back tears of anger.

"Can't you say anything, loser?" J.J. continued to jeer as Gump, Peanut, and Munchkin laughed.

"That's enough," Brad Cooper said, as he and Brett joined the conversation.

"We're just teasing old Stay Puff marshmallow man," J.J. smiled, as he reached over the handlebars and roughly squeezed the large boy. "You feel like super-sized silly putty."

"I said stop it!" Brad Cooper commanded.

Brad's tone of voice caused the other boys to stop laughing as J.J. turned his attention from Winkie Dink to Brad.

J.J. let go of the large boy and took a step toward Brad Cooper, "I was just having fun. Winkie Dink don't mind."

"His name is Jody," Brad said.

"Jody?" J.J. laughed while turning to look at the boy. "I think he likes Winkie Dink better."

The large boy did not respond, but Brad said, "His name is Jody Winkle and he shouldn't have to deal with a jerk like you."

J.J. Reynolds took another step toward Brad Cooper and said, "Who are you calling a jerk?"

Brad Cooper did not respond as J.J. Reynolds continued to approach.

"Who are you calling a jerk?" J.J. repeated loudly.

When Brad Cooper refused to reply, J.J. Reynolds pushed the round-faced Brad hard enough to cause him to stumble.

"Who are you calling a jerk?" J.J. shouted as he grabbed the off-balanced Brad Cooper.

"You," Brad calmly replied.

"You've gotten Winkie Dink off the hook," J.J. threatened, "because I'm about to show you a whole new level of beat down."

J.J. shoved Brad to the ground and menacingly stood over him.

"Get up," J.J. challenged.

Before Brad could get off the ground, Brett stepped in and said, "Maybe you want to shove me around?"

"What?" a confused J.J. asked.

"Get on home, Winkie—I mean Jody," Brett ordered.

Jody Winkle did not miss the opportunity to escape and quickly pedaled away from the group.

"You're taking Winkie Dink's side on this?" J.J. challenged.

"I didn't take a side," Brett sighed. "But you're not fighting Coop. If you want to fight, let's make it a good one—you and me."

J.J. Reynolds sized up Brett Bennett for a moment. J.J. stood a couple of inches taller, but Brett was faster and thicker.

"I can't fight you, B.B.," J.J. tried to explain. "It wouldn't be right."

"Then quit pushing Coop around," Brett sternly warned.

Brett turned around to help Brad Cooper to his feet when J.J. Reynolds lunged at him. Jordan watched as her brother spun J.J. to the ground. They wrestled for a few frantic seconds before Brett pinned J.J. with his forearm at his throat.

"Get off me!" J.J. screamed.

"Will you settle down?" Brett calmly asked.

J.J. Reynolds struggled for an instant until he could tell that he was trapped. He nodded his compliance. Brett let go and helped J.J. get to his feet.

"You okay Coop?" Brett asked.

Brad Cooper nodded his head.

Looking back at J.J. Reynolds, Brett asked, "How about you?"

An uncharacteristically meek J.J. Reynolds nodded as well.

"Still friends?" Brett asked.

"Yeah," J.J. muttered.

"Coop?" Brett asked.

"Yeah," Brad Cooper confirmed.

"Let's get home, Jordan," Brett said, as he gently nudged his younger sister toward the gate.

Jordan and Brett had walked about ten steps when J.J. Reynolds asked, "You coming tomorrow to play ball?"

Brett looked at J.J. Reynolds for a second and said, "Sure. I'll be there."

With his more typical bravado, J.J. Reynolds said, "You better."

Brett nodded and walked away quietly with Jordan.

The two walked silently for half a block before Jordan asked, "What's wrong?"

"Huh?" Brett responded.

"Something's bothering you," Jordan observed. "You haven't said a word."

"Nothing," Brett said. "Just thinking."

"About what?" Jordan prodded.

Brett thought for a moment and answered, "I guess I'm not feeling that great about myself right now."

"Why not?" Jordan asked. "You had J.J. pinned to the ground. I've never seen him so scared. I think you could take him easy."

"It's not that," Brett replied. "It's Jody."

"Winkie Dink?" Jordan asked.

"Yeah," Brett affirmed. "Everyone picks on him."

"He's annoying," Jordan observed.

"I know," Brett confirmed. "It must be hard being him, though. He's pretty much everyone's target at school. I think that's why he likes to pester you junior high kids."

"You've never bothered him," Jordan said.

"I've never picked on him, but I've stood by while others did," Brett sighed. "Like Gump and Peanut and Munchkin back there. They weren't doing anything wrong either, but they sure weren't doing anything right. Coop—Coop stood up for him. I didn't. I didn't step in until J.J. picked on Coop."

"Why did Brad do that?" Jordan asked. "I didn't know he even knew Winkie Dink."

"Better not call him Winkie Dink in front of Brad now," Brett smiled.

"Still," Jordan continued. "I didn't know they were friends."

"That's just it," Brett said. "They're not friends. Coop just stood up and did the right thing while I stood by and watched."

"Maybe you can be a stand-up guy some other time," Jordan suggested.

Brett smiled at his wide-eyed sister and replied, "Maybe so."

Brett took a longer look at this sister and asked, "Exactly what are you doing with that cat?"

"I'm taking care of it for a few days," Jordan explained. "The boys were picking on it and the lady that takes care of it is away for a few days."

Brett grunted and said, "Now my little sister is taking care of bullies just like Coop."

"I'm just taking care of the cat," Jordan clarified.

"Does Mom know?" Brett asked.

Jordan shook her head.

Brett laughed and said, "Looks like I may see one more fight tonight."

CHAPTER 31

The cat rested comfortably in Jordan's arms as she and Brett made their way onto 13th Street. The cat made no effort to escape, but Jordan was nervous as she approached her house. She had asked for a puppy when she first moved to Ponca City, but her mother had stubbornly refused to let her take care of one. A cat would be different, Jordan reasoned. Lydie Marland had once told her that cats did not really belong to anyone. Jordan could give the poor thing a little food and some attention, until Mrs. Marland returned to her cottage.

Three houses from home, Jordan's heart sank, as she gingerly put the cat down. The familiar pickup truck belonging to Mr. Reynolds was parked out front with a sheriff's car sitting behind it. Jordan's mother stood fearfully on the front porch as two men talked to her.

"Stay here," Brett said, as he trotted ahead to his mother.

Jordan stood on the street for a moment before deciding to see what was happening at the house. Jordan walked slowly toward her mother with the cat trailing quietly behind her. Jordan could not hear everything, but she could tell the conversation was about the rent and she heard the word "eviction process" used by Mr. Reynolds as the deputy stood next to him.

Jordan hurt inside to see her mother having to explain why the rent had been late so many times the past months. The street was empty, except for Mr. Grumman who stood stoically on his front porch watching the proceedings. Jordan pretended not to notice any of the activity as she slipped behind the house to the back door. The cat nearly followed her into the house, until Jordan noticed her trailing behind.

"Stay here," Jordan instructed. "I'll try to find some milk."

Jordan shut the door and saw Brett listening at the front door.

"What's going on?" Jordan whispered.

"What do you think?" Brett frowned. "We're being evicted."

"What does that mean?" Jordan asked, although she feared she knew the answer.

"It means we're out on the street," Brett informed her.

Brett muttered a few curses under his breath, which was uncharacteristic for him. Most of his anger was directed at his father, who had not come through with his promised child support payment.

"What are we going to do?" Jordan worriedly asked.

"I don't know," Brett admitted. "Do you have any cash?"

"Ten dollars," Jordan replied. "I've given the rest to Mom."

"Me too," Brett sighed. "Hope you like Mom's Omni."

"I don't," Jordan said.

"Too bad," Brett solemnly replied. "I think that's where you'll be sleeping for a few days."

Before Jordan could pry additional information from her brother, the front door opened and the two children pretended they had not been eavesdropping.

"Is everything okay?" Brett finally asked.

Jordan expected her mother to cry, but Barbara was detached and unemotional.

Barbara Bennett calmly replied, "We're being evicted. I've got two weeks to find us another place before the sheriff comes to put a padlock on this place and make us leave."

"What are we going to do?" an anxious Brett asked.

"We'll have to find another place," Barbara Bennett bravely replied. "We'll need to have a yard sale next weekend and get rid of anything we don't absolutely need. I'll scrape up what money I can and try to get your father to send the money he owes me in a money order."

"We'll find something," Barbara tried to assure them. "I've got two more months of school and then things will get better. We just have to find some place we can afford until then. We may be cramped, but we'll manage."

Barbara Bennett forced herself to smile, which helped Jordan believe things would work out. Brett stepped over and gave his mother a hug before retreating to his room.

"How did your day go?" Barbara Bennett asked her daughter.

"Fine," Jordan replied.

"Fine?" Barbara repeated. "What made it fine?"

"I guess it wasn't exactly fine," Jordan admitted. "I went to see Linda after school."

"Really?" Barbara said. "Should you have asked?"

"I would have," Jordan said. "But Linda's been gone all week from school and I was worried about her. I couldn't call or anything."

Barbara Bennett winced slightly at the reminder that she had not been able to pay the phone bill.

"I just needed to see her," Jordan quickly continued. "I took the bus and it wasn't that far to walk home."

"You walked all the way from Linda's?" Barbara quizzed.

Jordan nodded and continued, "Linda's got diabetes."

"Oh no," Barbara Bennett gasped. "What kind?"

"Regular, I guess," Jordan answered.

"Is she taking any medicine?" Barbara asked.

Jordan nodded and replied, "She has to get shots at least twice a day."

"Insulin," Barbara moaned.

"That's it," Jordan confirmed. "Is it bad, Mother?"

Barbara looked at her daughter and said, "It's not good, but at least they know what's going on with her now. Her mother must be worried sick."

"How long until Linda's well?" Jordan asked.

Barbara frowned and said, "Linda will always have to live with her diabetes. She'll be able to control it with her medicine, but once you take insulin, you have to keep taking it."

"Will she be okay?" Jordan worriedly asked.

"She'll be fine," Barbara tried to assure her anxious daughter.

Jordan bit her bottom lip and said, "I've got some more news."

Barbara raised her eyebrow and asked, "Yes?"

Jordan stepped to the back door to show her mother the cat on the back step.

"Jordan!" Barbara scolded. "You can't have a cat."

"It's not mine," Jordan reasoned. "It just followed me home."

Barbara looked unconvinced, as Jordan added, "Some boys were teasing it and it was so afraid. Can I just take care of it a few days and then I'll take it back to the mansion?"

"You brought this thing all the way from the Marland Mansion?" Barbara quizzed.

Jordan nodded and lied, "It followed me most of the way."

"Get it some milk for tonight, but I won't have it in my house," Barbara stated.

Barbara looked at the walls of their front room and said, "The cat shouldn't get too used to this house anyway. The new tenants might not like it around, and I'm sure we won't be able to have a pet when we move."

"Yes, ma'am," Jordan conceded.

Jordan looked at her mother a moment before asking, "Is there anything I can do to help?"

Barbara looked at her daughter and said, "You've done enough, sweetheart. I'm sorry I've let things get so behind."

"Brett says Daddy hasn't done his part," Jordan told her.

Barbara tried to muster the composure to make a civil response when she said, "Brett's angry right now and maybe he should be. We'll have to make the best of things."

Jordan nodded, although she knew Brett had been right. Her father had not done anything to make life easier for her the past year.

"You can do one thing," Barbara finally said. "Next time you go to clean Mr. Grumman's house, let him know we'll be moving. Tell him you appreciate the job, but I don't see how I can get you back here every week. He'll understand, I'm sure, but it's a good habit to let your employer know when you're going to leave with proper notice."

"I'll let him know," Jordan assured her.

"I'm sure that won't break your heart," Barbara smiled.

"It hasn't been bad," Jordan confessed. "I've kinda got used to Mr. Grumman."

"That shows some good work ethic," Barbara coached. "I appreciate you making the best out of the situation. Now, go feed that cat."

Jordan obeyed her mother and enjoyed watching the cat lap up her milk.

"You were hungry," Jordan whispered to the cat.

The cat did not acknowledge her, but Jordan patted the cat's soft neck and felt somehow satisfied to think the cat listened to her. Jordan knew she would not be able to keep the cat, but enjoyed taking care of her this night.

"She said your name was Florence," Jordan whispered to the cat. "I don't know why they called you Florence? That's not a cat name. It's more like a little old lady name."

The cat seemed to agree as she took a break from her milk to nuzzle Jordan's hand. Jordan continued to hold a one-sided conversation with the cat until her mother made her come inside. Jordan looked around her small backyard with a feeling of sadness. Jordan had not noticed when this place became her home. Now that she was faced with the uncertainty of moving, she was beginning to miss it. She petted the orphaned cat one last time and retreated to her small room to be alone with her thoughts.

CHAPTER 32

Mr. Grumman became more personable as he got used to having Jordan in his house, but he still represented an intimidating presence to the young girl. Jordan did not look forward to telling him she would need to quit.

Jordan cleaned the kitchen while Mr. Grumman read a magazine in the front room. She put things in order and glanced around the corner to see Mr. Grumman had fallen asleep in his chair. Jordan did not want to bother the old man so she double-checked her work before taking a moment to look outside. The odd looking markers she had seen in the backyard the past months drew her attention. She debated only a moment before slipping out of the house to take a look.

The grass had a teasing hint of green as Jordan walked slowly toward the grayish-white stones. The high wood fence surrounding the yard completely concealed the odd selection of marble Mr. Grumman had collected. Jordan stopped dead still in the middle of the yard when she realized the two strange stones that looked like tombstones were actually tombstones. The markers, one slightly larger than the other, stood solemnly in the solitude of Mr. Grumman's backyard. Jordan quickly looked back to the house to see she was alone before stepping closer.

Jordan knelt down to whisper, "Laura Grumman...born November 3, 1905 died January 26, 1951...Loving Wife and Mother."

Looking at the smaller stone, Jordan read, "Mellissa Grumman...born March 3, 1934 died January 26, 1951, Beloved Daughter."

Jordan reached out and gently touched the smooth and weathered smaller stone. It suddenly occurred to Jordan that she was standing on the grave of the young woman. Jordan straightened up to return to the house. As she turned to walk back, she yelped slightly when she saw Mr. Grumman staring coldly at her through the kitchen window. Jordan wanted to run away, but the only gate she saw was padlocked and the fence was much too high for her to climb.

As Mr. Grumman watched her, she walked slowly to the house to face her punishment. Mr. Grumman's expressionless face was stoically framed in the window.

Jordan opened the door intending to apologize, but before she could say anything, Mr. Grumman sighed, "That must seem odd to you—gravestones in a backyard."

"Your wife and daughter?" Jordan deduced.

"Yes," Mr. Grumman replied, as he gently shut the door.

"They're buried here?" Jordan asked.

Mr. Grumman seemed surprised by the question before saying, "No—no. They are laid to rest at the cemetery."

Jordan listened awkwardly. She could not think of anything to say so she decided to return to her work.

Before she left the room, however, Mr. Grumman continued, "They were killed in an automobile accident. January 26—January 26 is always a hard day for me. Melissa was a cheerleader. My wife drove her to a game in Enid on a Friday evening. I should have gone—I should have been there. They died that night and I wasn't there. They were my life and I wasn't there because I thought work was more important."

An uncomfortable Jordan muttered, "I'm sorry."

"It's so long ago, but I can never get them out of my mind," Mr. Grumman stated. "It's hard to explain to people."

"Why are the stones here?" Jordan asked.

Mr. Grumman stepped to the window and said, "I was a carver. That was my trade. I carved the stones, but after they were made, I decided they needed to be the same size. They weren't quite right for their place in the cemetery. I brought these here. That must seem crazy, but I liked having them here to remind me of how much I miss them both."

"I understand," Jordan offered.

"Really?" Mr. Grumman asked with a raised eyebrow.

"I guess not," Jordan confessed.

Mr. Grumman smiled slightly and said, "I learned to cut stone with a man that used to carve for the Marlands when they were building the mansion. I was a young man then and dreamed of being a sculptor."

"Are those some of your carvings?" Jordan asked, referring to several small statues in the backyard.

"Yes," Mr. Grumman sheepishly replied. "My hands won't let me work much these days, but I still like to carve. I had the ability to work in stone, but I never had the artist's eye. I made a good living carving gravestones and that allowed me to live here with Laura. We had a fine life. I got to see many great sculptors working for Mr. Marland. It was very exciting, but I was always happy with a life more ordinary."

Jordan asked, "Did you help with any of the carvings at the Mansion?"

Shaking his head, Mr. Grumman said, "Not really. I did some odd jobs, but I was young and it was more "go for" work. I got to do some polishing, but that was about as close as I got to sculpting anything for the mansion. You have to know that Mr. Marland brought in some of the best artisans in the world. I was just a young man that happened to live in town."

"But you knew Lydie Marland?" Jordan suggested.

Mr. Grumman nodded his head and replied, "We were close to the same age and both had artistic interest."

"What was she like?" Jordan asked.

"Lydie was shy," Mr. Grumman answered. "She still is, most would say. She went to a fine school back east and was very accomplished."

"Did she really marry her father?" Jordan sheepishly asked.

Mr. Grumman studied his young helper for a moment and said, "Poor Lydie. That was a part of her life that I'm not sure she was ever able to reconcile. Mr. Marland was not her real father, of course. She came to live here because the Marlands were very rich and her own family poor. Lydie was a shy girl and with her new found wealth, the Marlands always tried to protect her from people that might try to exploit her.

"Mr. Marland relied on Lydie for many things after his wife died. Lydie was twenty-six years old when she married him and from what I could see, she was happy. She was always more withdrawn from people than Mr. Marland. I think when he entered politics that made her even more suspicious."

"She seems so—odd," Jordan added. "I've only talked to her a few times, but she's not like anyone I've ever been around."

"You'll never meet anyone quite like Lydie Marland, I suspect," Mr. Grumman said. "She's unique. Have you seen Lydie lately?"

"No," Jordan said shaking her head. "Last time I saw her was in front of the library, but that was awhile back."

"Humm," Mr. Grumman sighed. "I haven't seen her in months, but I haven't been out much."

"I went by her place yesterday," Jordan shared. "Some boys were teasing her cat and I tried to return her. The neighbor said she had been ill and was away. Her cat followed me home and I guess I'll watch her a day or two."

"Lydie's so secretive, it's always been hard to know when she's home or away," Mr. Grumman said.

"I've wanted to see her," Jordan said.

"Really?" Mr. Grumman asked.

Jordan nodded, "I've wanted to ask her about—I've been curious about why she left town for so long and what she was doing during those years."

Mr. Grumman grunted a half-hearted laugh and said, "I wouldn't hold my breath. I think most people in town would like to know the answer to that question. I don't expect Lydie to tell, though."

"What do you think happened to her?" Jordan asked.

Mr. Grumman studied the inquisitive girl for a moment before thoughtfully saying, "I hear rumors, but I don't think much about rumors. I think she went away because she wanted to get away."

"Aren't you curious?" Jordan quizzed.

"I suppose," Mr. Grumman admitted. "But it's her life. I think it must have been hard—to be under so much scrutiny when all she wanted was to live peacefully. Lydie knows the reasons. Everything else is just speculation."

"I guess," Jordan sighed.

"You look like something else is on your mind," Mr. Grumman observed.

"My mother said I needed to give you notice that I won't be able to work," Jordan shared.

"What?" Mr. Grumman asked. "You've done a fine job as usual."

"Thank you," Jordan replied. "We're moving."

"Where to?" Mr. Grumman asked.

"I don't really know," Jordan confessed. "We're—I guess you saw the sheriff yesterday?"

Mr. Grumman nodded and said, "Your mother's still in school?"

"Yes, sir," Jordan answered. "She's close to finishing."

"She'll do well," Mr. Grumman stated. "She's got a healer's touch to her."

Jordan did not reply. She did not see her mother as particularly special in any way, but she did know her mother had been determined to stay in school, although the family's financial shortfall had challenged her resolve.

"She's anxious to finish," Jordan said, as she waited nervously to see if Mr. Grumman needed any other jobs done before she left.

"Here's your money," Mr. Grumman smiled, as he handed Jordan a twenty dollar bill.

Jordan looked at the money for a moment before saying, "I don't have change."

"You don't need it," Mr. Grumman replied. "You've done good work; I'm giving you a raise."

Jordan stared at the money without responding. She felt guilty for taking it. Mr. Grumman had never asked her to do anything but the simplest jobs and she did not think she deserved more. She had been giving the money she earned to her mother to help with the rent, and she knew any extra money would help.

"You better get home," Mr. Grumman suggested. "I'm sure you have things to do."

"Thank you," Jordan finally replied.

As Jordan stepped off the front porch, Mr. Grumman said, "Young lady, will you do something for me?"

Jordan nodded.

"Please have your mother come see me when she gets an opportunity," Mr. Grumman requested.

"Yes, sir," Jordan agreed.

Mr. Grumman watched the young girl walk quickly back to her house until she disappeared inside. He had noticed the house being dark the past few days and suspected the electric company had cut off the power again. He had wanted to do more for the family, but knew Barbara Bennett would not willingly accept anything resembling charity. There was more than an hour of daylight, and it caused him to frown knowing the girl would be sitting in the dark house when her mother returned.

CHAPTER 33

"Did Mr. Grumman say what he wanted?" Barbara Bennett asked, as she headed out the door to speak to the old man on the corner.

"No," Jordan assured.

"Keep busy," Barbara implored. "We've got to get ready to move. I want to be gone before the sheriff has to come back."

"Okay," Jordan nodded.

Barbara Bennett headed out the door wearing her scrubs from the clinical practice she had done earlier in the day. When her mother left, Jordan went to the back door to see if her new friend was there. The cat's throaty purr indicated she was ready to play. Barbara Bennett had reluctantly let her daughter feed the cat a few scraps and milk. Her mother had no idea that Jordan had let the feline be the Bennett house cat when she was away.

"How's my kitty?" Jordan asked as she cradled the cat in her arms.

Jordan felt a simple satisfaction in having a creature give her such full attention.

"Linda was back in school today," Jordan continued informing the cat. "We had a conversation at lunch about you. She wants to come see you before Mrs. Marland comes home."

The cat responded by gently rubbing its head against Jordan's arm. After a few more minutes Jordan decided not to test her luck and sent the cat to the backyard with a saucer of milk. Knowing her mother would soon return, Jordan frantically went through her drawers sorting through any clothes that might be too small. Barbara Bennett had warned her children that they would be living in a much smaller apartment, but Jordan was pretty sure that everything she owned would fit in a box, except for her old mattress.

A knock on the door interrupted Jordan's packing and she went to the front window to see Brad Cooper standing outside.

"Hey Jordan," Brad Cooper said, as the girl opened the door.

"Hi," Jordan replied.

"Is B.B. around?" he asked.

"No," Jordan said shaking her head. "I think he's at TG&Y until five."

"Oh," Brad said. "I forgot he was working today. Tell him I came by, if you would."

"Sure," Jordan said, as the boy stepped off the small porch.

"Coop!" Jordan yelped before the boy could mount his bicycle.

"Yeah," he replied before stepping back to the door.

"Why did you stand up for Winkie Dink the other day?" Jordan asked.

Brad blushed slightly and replied, "I don't know."

Jordan watched the boy for a moment in silence before Brad said, "I feel sorry for him sometimes."

Brad hesitated before saying, "That's not really it either. I'm the one that stuck him with the name Winkie Dink. We were at a camp a few years ago and Jody's one of those guys that's easy not to like—he tries way too hard. Back then we called everyone by their last name and a group of us were giving him a pretty hard time. Instead of saying Winkle, I said Winkie—pretty soon someone added Dink and the name stuck. Something about J.J. got to me that day. He's a—"

"Real jerk sometimes," Jordan interrupted.

Brad smiled at the observation and said, "Yeah—sometimes. J.J.'s all right, but he has this thing that he's got to put everyone else down. Your brother saved me that day."

"Brett was impressed with you," Jordan shared. "He told me so."

"Your brother's the best," Brad commented. "I guess you know that."

"Not always," Jordan admitted.

"I'll see you around, Jordan," Brad said. "I'll try to catch Brett when he gets off work."

Brad Cooper rode away on his bicycle and Jordan went back to her job of packing. She studied a stack of old school papers, trying to determine if they should be saved or tossed, when she heard her mother open the front door.

"Mom, do you want to save these?" Jordan asked, as she showed her mother some of the papers.

Barbara looked at her daughter strangely and replied, "You can keep them. In fact, you can quit packing things. We're staying."

"What?" Jordan asked.

"We're staying!" Barbara Bennett beamed.

"How?" Jordan questioned. "Did you find an envelope full of money on the street?"

"Almost," Barbara replied. "Mr. Grumman's taking care of things."

"Mr. Grumman gave you the rent money?" Jordan asked.

Jordan had developed a reasonable rapport with Mr. Grumman, but had not seen evidence of much generosity in his demeanor. He had been known as Mr. Grumpy and there had been good reason.

"Not exactly," Barbara explained. "It seems Mr. Grumman owns this house. He's our landlord. Mr. Reynolds manages this and several other properties for him."

"Mr. Grumman evicted us?" Jordan responded.

"He apologized," Barbara said. "He doesn't keep up with the properties himself and didn't know we were behind."

"So Mr. Grumman is just letting us stay for free?" Jordan questioned.

"Of course not," Barbara replied. "He knows we'll pay. I'll be out of school in a few weeks and I've already been offered a job at the hospital. It's a good job and we'll make it."

"That's great," Jordan smiled.

"He did ask me one question," Barbara continued. "He wants to know if you'll still come clean for him. He said you gave him notice. If you really don't want to work, you don't have to."

"I don't mind," Jordan assured her.

"Good," Barbara smiled.

"When do you think Brett will be home?" Barbara asked.

"In about an hour," Jordan guessed.

"Excellent," Barbara said. "I'm taking my kids out to eat tonight."

"Are you taking us to the Rusty Barrel?" Jordan joked.

The Rusty Barrel was a supper club featuring the best steaks in the city. Jordan had never eaten there, but the Bennett family always joked that they would eat there when their ship came in.

"No," Barbara chastised her. "It'll be McDonald's, but it will be a night out all the same."

"Sounds good," Jordan smiled.

"You have an hour," Barbara said. "Take that cat back before she gets too used to being here."

"But Mom, can't she stay a few more days?" Jordan pleaded. "I don't think Mrs. Marland will be back and it's a long walk."

"I don't care," Barbara ordered. "You have plenty of time."

Jordan was not happy, but did not want to challenge her mother more while she was in a good mood.

"Okay," Jordan sulked.

Without more prodding, Jordan went outside hoping she would not be able to find the visiting cat. Jordan was disappointed when the cat crouched outside the back door waiting for her.

"You really should have wandered off," Jordan scolded.

Jordan carried a large wicker basket she had found to carry the cat around. Reluctantly, Jordan gently put the cat in the basket and the cat seemed content to rest there. Jordan started north, but before she left the yard, she looked down the street at Mr. Grumman's house on the corner. She quickly detoured and headed south to thank her employer.

Jordan knocked on the door with much less trepidation than she had months earlier. She had gotten used to Mr. Grumman's gruff manner and had enjoyed hearing his stories about the past—particularly Lydie Marland.

In a moment, Mr. Grumman came to the door.

"Jordan?" Mr. Grumman greeted her, somewhat confused.

"Hi," Jordan replied.

"What are you doing here?" Mr. Grumman asked. "I didn't expect you until tomorrow."

"I didn't come to work," Jordan explained.

"Here for a visit?" Mr. Grumman suggested.

Jordan nodded.

"Why don't you come in," Mr. Grumman offered.

Jordan followed him into the front room and nervously took a seat across from the old man.

"What's in the basket?" he asked.

Jordan looked at the basket with the cat hiding inside and said, "It's a cat."

Coaxing the cat into her arms she continued, "She's Mrs. Marland's cat—I've been watching her for a few days, but Mom says I've got to take her back. I've kinda adopted her."

"Looks like she's adopted you," Mr. Grumman smiled, as he watched the cat nuzzle against the girl.

In a more serious tone, Mr. Grumman added, "You'll be wasting a trip to take her back. Lydie's been in the hospital."

"Oh no," Jordan moaned. "Is she okay?"

"She's been sick and needs more help than she can get at her place," Mr. Grumman explained. "She may be in the hospital for a while and will probably be in a care facility after that."

"I don't know about her cat then," Jordan said. "I found her the other day and some boys where teasing her. She followed me and I—I took her home."

"It's a good thing," Mr. Grumman replied. "She'll need someone to watch after her."

"Mrs. Marland said the cat couldn't be on her own," Jordan justified. "She said the cat had nearly starved when its previous owner moved away."

Taking a closer look at the cat, Mr. Grumman said, "I remember this cat. She was a pampered princess when she used to live at the Danielson's house. She was a scrawny thing when she took up with Lydie."

"Will she be okay?" Jordan asked.

"The cat?" Mr. Grumman replied.

"No," Jordan said shaking her head. "Mrs. Marland."

Mr. Grumman thought for a few seconds and said, "Lydie's tougher than people think. She's a survivor."

Looking at the cat still cradled in Jordan's arm, he continued, "Lydie's like this cat, I suppose. She was used to a lot and then it was all taken away. She learned to survive in her own way. This cat is lucky to have you."

"If Mom will let me keep her," Jordan frowned.

Mr. Grumman laughed and said, "If she won't, bring her to me and I'll let her chase my mice away."

Jordan smiled, knowing she had a back-up plan to take care of the cat.

"I really came to thank you," Jordan said, as she gently returned the cat to her basket.

With a raised eyebrow, Mr. Grumman said, "What for?"

"We're staying in our house," Jordan explained. "Mom says that wouldn't have happened without you."

Mr. Grumman shifted nervously in his chair and replied, "Oh, that."

"You don't know how much it means to us," Jordan said.

"It was nothing," Mr. Grumman apologized. "It was just a misunderstanding that had to be cleared up—nothing more."

"Mom says you own our house," a puzzled Jordan replied. "Mr. Reynolds was going to evict us—I'm sure you saw the sheriff's deputy the other day."

"I—I know," Mr. Grumman meekly admitted. "Mr. Reynolds does manage several properties I own. Mr. Reynolds is a very conscientious manager and he has his procedures. He should have talked to me before he took action."

"I don't understand," Jordan frowned.

"I've taken care of my money through the years," Mr. Grumman explained. "After my wife and daughter passed away, I got absorbed in my businesses. One of those was buying and fixing up old houses—at least when I was younger. I hired Mr. Reynolds several years ago to manage my property. He knows I'm a hard man and he's run things by the book. They don't call me Mr. Grumpy for nothing."

"You know about that?" Jordan timidly asked.

With a sly smile Mr. Grumman nodded and continued, "I've always been a bottom-line kind of person and the fact is I have more money than good neighbors. I like your mother's character. I know she'll pay when she gets things caught up a bit."

Mr. Grumman could tell his young visitor was not quite convinced so he added, "Your mother's the first person that's tried to do something nice for me in a long time. When I went into the hospital last year, she had your brother come and mow my yard."

"But he nearly ruined it," Jordan noted. "You can still see the stripes where he scalped your yard."

"That's true," Mr. Grumman smiled. "It's the thought that counts, though. Your mother takes responsibility—she won't allow herself to be a victim. This has been a hard year for your family, but I think things are going to turn around for you. If I have to wait an extra month for my rent money, I see that as a good investment. Besides, I couldn't very well have my best helper move away."

It took Jordan a few seconds to realize Mr. Grumman was referring to her.

"I guess not," Jordan replied.

Mr. Grumman looked at the young girl and said, "That cat's lucky to have you. We all need someone to care about us, and I can tell you're going to do a good job with that cat."

"I hope so," Jordan confessed.

Jordan said goodbye to Mr. Grumman and stepped to the porch to make the short walk home.

Mr. Grumman followed Jordan to the porch and said, "That's your cat now. I think you should choose a name."

"Mrs. Marland said her name was Florence," Jordan replied.

"That doesn't sound like a cat name," Mr. Grumman declared.

"What do you think I should call her?" Jordan asked.

Mr. Grumman thought for a moment and said, "I can't think of a good name, but I'm betting you'll think of something."

CHAPTER 34

Barbara Bennett graduated in a simple, but elegant ceremony from her nursing program in May. She won the Florence Nightingale award from her instructor and Brett thought to buy his mother roses for the occasion. Jordan proudly watched the pinning ceremony and admired her mother's perseverance. Barbara successfully completed her Board of Nursing exams, which resulted in a good job at the hospital. That year marked a positive turn around for the Bennett family. Jordan gave up on the ideal family she remembered and embraced what her family could become.

Jordan did not realize it at the time, but that was the year Ponca City became her home—she learned that any place could be home with the right attitude. In late July, a solemn Mr. Grumman informed Jordan that Lydie Marland had passed away. Jordan accompanied him to a memorial service held in the lower level of the great Marland Mansion with a few hundred people attending. Jordan listened to the kind words and stories others shared about the enigmatic woman who had lived with the extremes of wealth and poverty. Lydie Marland was remembered as a thoughtful, gracious, and thankful woman who guarded her privacy and lived on her own terms.

Jordan had her own memories of the eccentric woman, but left the funeral with a nagging curiosity she now believed would never be satisfied.

"Is this your first funeral?" Mr. Grumman asked, as he walked with her into the hot summer afternoon.

Jordan nodded, somberly.

"It was a nice service," Mr. Grumman added.

"It was depressing," Jordan responded.

"People die every day," Mr. Grumman shared. "It's a fact of life."

"I know," Jordan sighed. "It's just—"

After a moment's hesitation, Mr. Grumman coaxed, "It's just what?"

"All of the questions—the mystery," Jordan confessed. "I wanted to know why she went away. I wanted to know what she did all those years. I wished I had just asked her when I had the chance."

Mr. Grumman smiled and said, "It wouldn't have mattered. Lydie would never tell why she went away—I'm not sure she knew herself. A person's got to be true to themselves. Lydie lost that part of herself somewhere along the way and spent years trying to find it."

"It's all so sad," Jordan reflected.

"Why's that?" Mr. Grumman asked.

"Her life," Jordan explained. "She lost everything."

"Did she ever seem sad when you were around her?" Mr. Grumman questioned.

"No," Jordan confessed. "She was—odd sometimes and seemed annoyed by my questions, but I wouldn't say she was sad."

"Lydie was suspicious of people," Mr. Grumman noted. "Maybe even a little paranoid some would say. I think Lydie wanted to be left alone—in the end that's what she got. Her tragedy may be that she was brought into a world of unlimited wealth and expectations—not what she lost."

"Maybe," Jordan replied. "She did seem content to enjoy a nice day with her cat when I would see her around this place."

"Speaking of which," Mr. Grumman asked. "Did you ever name the cat?"

Jordan nodded and said, "She always seems to slip around and hide from me. I never know what she's really up to or thinking. Whenever I look for her, she can't be found and then from nowhere, she'll appear—like a ghost. I call her Lydie's Ghost."

Mr. Grumman chuckled, as he unlocked the door of his Buick for the short drive home and commented, "That's a perfect name. I've watched the old cat sneak around myself from the front porch, and I think Lydie's Ghost has a lot of Lydie Marland's personality in her."

Jordan returned to the comfort of her air-conditioned house and found Lydie's Ghost lying comfortably in her favorite corner. Barbara Bennett first insisted that Jordan could not have a pet and then demanded the animal be kept outside. After a few weeks, however, Lydie's Ghost became the queen of the house, going when she wanted and where she wanted.

Jordan continued cleaning Mr. Grumman's house through high school. When the Bennett family moved away from 13th Street a few years later, Jordan drove the old Dodge Omni to his house. Mr. Grumman paid well and Jordan always spent a few minutes visiting with him when she would finish. He would ask about Jordan's pet and they often discussed their memories of the secretive Lydie Marland.

Mr. Grumman was ninety-two years old when he was forced to go to a local nursing home. Jordan was determined to visit every week, but he only lasted a few days in the home. Barbara Bennett explained that it was his time and Jordan thought she understood.

Brett developed into a standout football player in high school and received a scholarship to play college football at Harding University in Arkansas leaving Jordan to live alone with her mother for a couple of years. A few weeks before Jordan prepared to go to college herself, Lydie's Ghost disappeared. Barbara Bennett believed the old cat had gone off to die, but Jordan always kept an eye out for her old friend. Jordan often found herself walking around the Marland Mansion and believed she would someday find Lydie's Ghost there.

Linda Pelletier became Jordan's best friend throughout high school. Jordan had wanted to follow her brother to Harding, but Linda's parents wanted her closer to home and Linda convinced Jordan to be her roommate at Oklahoma

Christian in Oklahoma City. Mr. Pelletier was an Oklahoma State man, but he liked that the small school locked the girls in the dorm at 11:15 at night and had room checks.

Jordan earned a partial scholarship and was working on her financial aid to attend school when she learned Mr. Grumman had set up a college fund for her before he passed away. Jordan and Linda were roommates for two years until Linda married a youth minister and moved to Texas. Jordan returned to Ponca City for the summer in 1993 to a buzz of excitement. The limestone statue of Lydie Marland had been found. The stone carving was in many pieces, but there were plans to try to restore it to its former glory.

As Jordan watched the statue take form, she remembered her brief encounters with the gracious and eccentric Lydie Marland. Jordan, however, thought more about Mr. Grumman, his love of carving, and how much he would have enjoyed seeing the statue repaired. Jordan often walked the grounds of the Marland Mansion and reflected on its impact on her life.

Jordan ran into J.J. Reynolds on one of her trips back to Ponca City. The brash young man had matured somewhat. He was still handsome with a requisite amount of the old arrogance she remembered. J.J. asked about his old friend Brett, but he seemed more interested in her, although Jordan knew they shared nothing more than a few childhood escapades. J.J. Reynolds told her Brad Cooper had returned to Ponca City to work as an engineer at the refinery, but Jordan already knew. She and Brad had been taking long walks around the Marland Mansion for many months and were planning a wedding at the mansion in the fall.

In the evenings, Jordan would stroll around the old mansion remembering adventures from her past, but planning memories for the future. She always felt an odd aura when at the mansion—a sense something great and mysterious was always possible. Some people believed Lydie Marland's presence could still be felt at the Palace on the Prairie where she had once been the princess. Lydie Marland once said, "The Marland Mansion was a place that was naturally emotional and personal—a place of rare beauty and artistic integrity—a structure that is an expression from mind into substance, of the quality, the strength, and the heart of a man."

Jordan had named her stray cat Lydie's Ghost in childish whimsy, but as she walked the grounds of the enchanted mansion she knew the real Lydie watched over the place as if it was eternally hers. Jordan knew it was.

THE END

If you enjoyed *Lydie's Ghost*, look for these other Bob Perry novels:

The Broken Statue
Mimosa Lane
Brothers of the Cross Timber
Guilt's Echo
The Nephilim Code

www.bobp.biz

Lydie Marland: Oklahoma's Anastasia
An Essay

The puzzle of Lydie Marland's life haunts anyone who has been captivated by her extraordinary story. Lydie has been described as mysterious, eccentric, beautiful, artistic, refined, enigmatic, and troubled. She was called a "Princess" when she became the first lady of Oklahoma. I'm sure she was called many other things—good and bad—by those who thought they knew her. The Marland story is fantastic to the point of unbelievable, and Lydie's part in the legend is perhaps the most tragic.

Lydie's Ghost is the second novel I've written based loosely on the life of Lydie Marland. I did not become aware of her story until nearly twelve years after her death. The generation that would have known the real Lydie will someday be gone, and we are left with the stories about this fascinating woman. I personally did not know Lydie, but her story has always been too compelling for me to leave alone. As I've talked to various groups in promoting my first fictional novel, *The Broken Statue*, I have witnessed the fascination people have with this remarkable woman. I have always tried to depict her in an honorable and respectful manner. I truly hope I have been able to do that.

Most people interested in Lydie's legacy never knew the real Lydie and most that have some memories of her knew an elderly woman that must have appeared somewhat eccentric. Like me, they have learned about the extraordinary woman by the stories told by others. I have met a few people that actually interacted with the real Lydie Marland. One man I remember particularly came to a book signing I held in Ponca City. The gentleman was older and wore overalls. He did not look like the typical bookstore customer, but he stood in line anyway with his copy of *The Broken Statue* tucked under his arm. When I greeted him, I asked if he was familiar with the Marland story and he said he was. He went on to tell me that he had met the real Lydie when she was in her mid-twenties—he was eleven or twelve years old at the time. Obviously, I was supremely interested in talking to anyone who had actually witnessed any part of Lydie's life. The man explained that he was just a boy and would see her around town. He went on to say that he had quite a "crush on her" as a young boy. I asked the man how long that lasted and he said, "to this day."

The facts about Lydie Marland's life are well documented. She was born Lydie Roberts in Flourtown, Pennsylvania outside of Philadelphia. The family was middle-class at best. Lydie and her older brother George came to Ponca City around 1912 to visit their aunt, Virginia Marland. E.W. and Virginia Marland were unable to have children, so Lydie and George were eventually adopted by them around 1916. The family lived in a large mansion surrounded by eight acres of manicured gardens.

E.W. Marland founded an oil company that eventually became Conoco Oil and later Conoco/Phillips. It is estimated that E.W. Marland controlled 10% of the world's oil production in the early 1920s. Lydie became a debutante, attended the finest schools, and had the best of everything life could offer. By the mid 1920s, E.W. Marland decided to build a lavish mansion on a hill at the edge of Ponca City that would be a showcase for the world. At the time it was the largest single residential home west of the Mississippi River. Virginia Marland battled a long illness that resulted in her death in the summer of 1926. Work on Marland's great mansion continued even as his grip on the control of his oil company was slipping away.

On July 14, 1928 Lydie Marland had a most astonishing day. She began the day as Miss Lydie Marland, had her adoption of twelve years annulled to become Lydie Roberts, and then the twenty-eight year old Lydie married her former adopted father to become Mrs. Lydie Marland. This extraordinary day was followed by an extended honeymoon. By the time the newlywed Mr. and Mrs. Marland arrived back in Ponca City, E.W. Marland's oil company was nearly lost.

Even before the onset of The Great Depression, E.W. Marland's dream of living a long and peaceful life in the new mansion he had built began to crumble. By the early thirties, much of Marland's former wealth disappeared.

E.W. Marland was not a person content to live a life anywhere close to ordinary. In 1932 he was elected as congressman for north central Oklahoma. The Marlands spent two years in Washington before E.W. Marland became the 10th governor of Oklahoma on January 14, 1935. E.W. Marland with Lydie as first lady served as governor during the bleakest days of the state's great Dust Bowl and economic depression. E.W. Marland ran for the United States Senate twice, but was unable to win. He and Lydie moved back to Ponca City, and in October of 1941 E.W. Marland died leaving behind his forty-one year old widow.

The next chapter of Lydie's mysterious life started her journey toward being the reclusive woman many remember. Still a beautiful woman, Lydie more or less assumed a simpler and less public life. Her desire for secrecy erupted in 1953 when she abruptly left town. For nearly twenty-two years, Lydie Marland disappeared and few if any knew anything concerning her whereabouts. In 1958, the *Saturday Evening Post* published an article entitled "Where is Lyde Marland" that fueled speculation about her location, well-being, and state of mind. Lydie Marland slipped back into Ponca City in the mid-1970s and vigorously protected her privacy.

Lydie Marland passed away in the summer of 1987 at eighty-seven years old. Many viewed her as odd, eccentric, or peculiar. Lydie's missing years and life have spawned a myriad of theories about her motivations, but few, if any, know the real reasons—some believe even Lydie did not know. I suspect Lydie did not understand why people were fascinated by her extraordinary experiences.

Like many, I have ideas about what the real Lydie was like without knowing for certain. I do know her story continues to interest people and believe it will for many years to come. I've always thought Lydie probably would have enjoyed a life more ordinary. I believe she loved her husband. E.W. Marland was a man that lived large and would not have been content with an ordinary life. Lydie's burden was to live her life under the considerable shadow cast by the spotlight on her husband's life.

I've often thought of Lydie as Oklahoma's Anastasia. Lydie was actually one year older than the Grand Duchess of Russia. Like Anastasia, Lydie disappeared from sight and stimulated years of speculation. As many waited for Anastasia to resurface and claim her rightful place in history, people also anticipated Lydie Marland's return for many years. Unlike Anastasia, Lydie did come home to live out the rest of her life in the hometown that had seen her enjoy good times and bad. Lydie lived out the sunset years of her life overlooking the great Marland Mansion that E.W. Marland had called the Palace on the Prairie. She must have looked at the great house with intense feelings of pride and sadness.

I believe E.W. Marland loved Ponca City, and I have become a great admirer of his accomplishments in business and as governor of Oklahoma. E.W. Marland had many opportunities to take his fortune and go somewhere else, yet stayed in Ponca City to the end of his life. Lydie, I feel, had a love-hate relationship with the place. In the end, I hope she made her peace with her home and her life.

The monuments left by E.W. Marland are everywhere in the city and state he helped form. The image of Lydie found in a statue carved when she was the princess of the Marland Empire was rescued after she had ordered it destroyed. The restored statue graces the entrance to the Marland Mansion to greet visitors that still come to marvel at the remarkable house and story. Lydie Marland always saw E.W. Marland as an exceptional man—we can only hope Lydie understood how special she was.

Made in the USA
Columbia, SC
22 December 2020

29562204R00167